W9-BNX-894

Fair Warning

ALSO BY ROBERT OLEN BUTLER

The Alleys of Eden

Sun Dogs

Countrymen of Bones

On Distant Ground

Wabash

The Deuce

A Good Scent from a Strange Mountain

They Whisper

Tabloid Dreams

The Deep Green Sea

Mr. Spaceman

Fair Warning

a novel

ROBERT
OLEN
BUTLER

Atlantic Monthly Press
New York

Copyright © 2002 by Robert Olen Butler

All rights reserved. No part of this book may be reproduced in any form or by
any electronic or mechanical means, including information storage and
retrieval systems, without permission in writing from the publisher, except by
a reviewer, who may quote brief passages in a review. Any members of
educational institutions wishing to photocopy part or all of the work for
classroom use, or publishers who would like to obtain permission to include
the work in an anthology, should send their inquiries to Grove/Atlantic, Inc.,
841 Broadway, New York, NY 10003.

Published simultaneously in Canada
Printed in the United States of America

FIRST EDITION

Library of Congress Cataloging-in-Publication Data

Butler, Robert Olen.
Fair warning : a novel / Robert Olen Butler.
p. cm.
ISBN 0-87113-833-6
1. Auctioneers—Fiction.   2. Art—Collectors and collecting—Fiction.
3. Americans—France—Fiction.   4. New York (N.Y.)—Fiction.
5. Paris (France)—Fiction.   I. Title.
PS3552.U8278 F35 2002

813'.54—dc21   2001022523

Atlantic Monthly Press
841 Broadway
New York, NY 10003

02 03 04 05   10 9 8 7 6 5 4 3 2 1

For Elizabeth Dewberry,
my wife and best friend

Acknowledgments

My sincere thanks is owed to a number of people who made this book possible. First to Francis Ford Coppola for hiring me to pursue his idea of creating a story around a female auctioneer. And to Sharon Stone for inspiring Francis. To Adrienne Brodeur, a remarkable editor who richly deserves the honors that have come to *Zoetrope: All Story*, where *Fair Warning* first appeared in story form. To my splendid agents, Kim Witherspoon in New York and Michael Siegel and Priscilla Cohen in L.A. And, of course, to Morgan Entrekin for his brilliant editorial guidance, and to all the other folks at Grove/Atlantic, who still care deeply about literary fiction. Thanks, too, to Bruce Cockburn, whose music has long nurtured my vision of things, and to my son, Joshua, whose own wonderful work has begun. And a special thanks to Betsy, without whom my words would have blurred into mumbling some time ago.

Fair Warning

Perhaps my fate was sealed when I sold my three-year-old sister. My father had taken me to a couple of cattle auctions, not minding that I was a girl—this was before Missy was born, of course—and I'd loved the fast talk and the intensity of the whole thing. So the day of my seventh birthday party, where Missy did a song for everyone while I sat alone, my chin on my hand, and meditated behind my still uncut birthday cake, it seemed to me that here was a charming and beautiful little asset I had no further use for and that could be liquidated to good effect. The next day I gathered a passel of children from our gated community in Houston, kids with serious money, and I had Missy do a bit of her song once more, and I said, "Ladies and gentlemen, no greater or more complete perfection of animal beauty ever stood on two legs than the little girl who stands before you. She has prize-winning breeding and good teeth. She will neither hook, kick, strike nor bite you. She is the pride and joy and greatest treasure of the Dickerson family and she is now available to you. Who will start the bidding for this future blue ribbon winner? Who'll offer fifty cents? Fifty cents. Who'll give me fifty?" I saw nothing but blank stares before me. I'd gotten all these kids together but I still hadn't quite gotten them into the spirit of the thing. So I looked one of these kids in the eye and I said, "You, Tony Speck. Aren't your parents rich enough to give you an allowance of fifty cents?" He made a hard, scrunched-up face and he said, "A dollar." And I was off. I finally sold her for six dollars and twenty-five cents to a quiet girl up the street whose daddy was in oil. She was an only child, a thing I made her feel sorry about when the bidding slowed down at five bucks.

Needless to say, the deal didn't go through. Missy tried to go get her dolls and clothes before she went off to what I persuaded her was a happy, extended sleep over, and Mama found out. That night my parents and Missy ate dinner in the dining room and I was put in my own room upstairs with a TV tray to eat my spaghetti alone. If I wanted to sell any one of them, then I wanted to sell them all, they claimed, and eating alone was supposed to show me how it would feel. I was supposed to be lonely. Of course, they were wrong. It was just my sister I wanted to dispose of. And all I was feeling was that somehow Missy had done it to me again. She was at my daddy's elbow downstairs, offering her cheek for pinching. I felt pissed about that but I also felt exhilarated at the thought of what I'd done at the sale. I figured she wasn't worth even half the final bid.

I am forty years old. Recently turned, and it's true I don't look it. But splendid condition—and enchanting provenance—notwithstanding, an object also is what it is by its objective standards. I'm forty now. Missy is thirty-six. My daddy is dead. For more than a year. Mama sits in the same rambling faux Queen Anne on the same gated street in Houston.

And I'm sure she continues to wonder why her two daughters have chosen to live seventeen hundred miles away. She's long wondered that, though she's always been forgiving of Missy because there was a husband involved. As for me, I still feel exhilarated when I can sell something to somebody, especially when they end up valuing the thing more than anyone else possibly could. Perhaps in some way *all* our fates were sealed.

Still, these past weeks following my fortieth birthday have been, at the very least, unexpected. It started with the Crippenhouse auction. Near the end of the morning, after I'd gaveled down dozens of lots of major artwork for big money from a big crowd that nearly filled our Blue Salon, a tiny, minor Renoir came up. Barely six inches square. One fat naked young woman with a little splash of vague foliage behind her. Generic Impressionism on a very small scale. Like a nearsighted man looking through the knothole in a fence without his glasses. And yet I stood before these wealthy people and I knew them well, most of them, knew them from playing them at this podium many times before and meeting them at parties and studying the social registers and reading their bios and following their ups and downs and comings and goings in the society columns and the *Wall Street Journal* and even the *Times* news pages. I stood before them and there was a crisp smell of ozone in the air and the soft clarity of our indirect lights and, muffled in our plush drapery and carpeting, the rich hush of money well and profusely spent. I looked around, giving them a moment to catch their breath. The estimate on the Renoir was one hundred and forty thousand dollars. Often we'd put a relatively low estimate on a thing we knew would be hot in order to draw in more sharks looking for an easy kill, and if you knew what you were doing, they wouldn't even realize that you'd actually gotten them into a feeding frenzy until they'd done something foolish. But this was one of those items where we'd jacked up the estimate on a minor piece that had one prestige selling point in order to improve its standing. Renoir. He's automatically a big deal, we were saying. In fact, though, we were going to be happy getting eighty percent of the estimate. I had just one bid in the book lying open before me—mine was bound in Morocco with gilt pages—which is where an auctioneer notes the order bids, the bids placed by the big customers with accounts who are too busy sunning themselves somewhere in the Mediterranean or cutting deals down in Wall Street to attend an auction. For the little Renoir, the one book bid wasn't even six figures, and I knew the guy had a thing for fat women.

So I looked out at the bid-weary group and I said, "I know you people," though at the moment I said this, my eyes fell on a man on the far left side about eight rows back who, in fact, I did not know. There were, of course, others in the room I didn't know, but this man had his eyes on me and he was as small-scaled and indistinct to my sight as the fat girl in the painting. But he was fixed on me and I could see his eyes were dark and his hair was dark and slicked straight back and his jaw was quite square and I know those aren't enough things to warrant being caught stopping and looking at somebody and feeling some vague sense of possibility—no, hardly even that—feeling a surge of heat in your brow and a little catch and then quickening of your breath.

I forced my attention to the matter at hand. "I know you," I repeated, getting back into the flow that had already started in me. "You're wearing hundred-dollar underpants and carrying thousand-dollar fountain pens."

They laughed. And they squirmed a little. Good.

I said, "You will not relinquish even the smallest detail of your life to mediocrity."

Now they stirred. I am known for talking to my bidders. Cajoling them. Browbeating them, even. At Christie's and Sotheby's they would grumble at what I do. But they value me at Nichols and Gray for these things. And my regulars here know what to expect.

I said, "But there is a space in the rich and wonderful place where you live that is given over to just such a thing, mediocrity. A square column in the foyer, a narrow slip of wall between two doors. You know the place. Think about it. Feel bad about it. And here is Pierre-Auguste Renoir, dead for eighty years, the king of the most popular movement in the history of serious art, ready to turn that patch of mediocrity into a glorious vision of corporeal beauty. Lot 156. Entitled 'Adorable Naked French Woman with Ample Enough Thighs to Keep Even John Paul Gibbons in One Place.'" And with this I looked directly at John Paul Gibbons, who was in his usual seat to the right side in the second row. He was as famous in the world of these people for his womanizing as for his money. I said, "Start the bidding at forty thousand, John Paul."

He winked at me and waved his bidder's paddle and we were off.

"Forty thousand," I said. "Who'll make it fifty?"

Since John Paul was on my right, I suppose it was only natural for me to scan back to the left to draw out a competing bid. I found myself looking toward the man with the dark eyes. How had I missed this face all morning? And he raised his paddle.

"Fifty thousand . . . " I cried and I almost identified him in the way I'd been thinking of him, as "Dark Eyes." But I caught myself. ". . . to the gentleman on the left side." I was instantly regretful for having started this the way I had. Was Renoir's pudgy beauty his type?

My auctioneer self swung back to John Paul Gibbons to pull out a further bid, even as the thoughts of another, covert self in me raced on.

"Sixty from Mr. Gibbons," I said, thinking, If she is his type, then I'm shit out of luck. All my life I've been in desperate pursuit of exactly the wrong kind of butt.

And sure enough, Dark Eyes bid seventy. I was happy for womanhood in general, I guess, if this were true, that men were coming back around to desiring the likes of this plumped-up pillow of a young woman, but I was sad for me, and I looked over my shoulder at her and my auctioneer self said, "Isn't she beautiful?" and my voice betrayed no malice.

John Paul took it to eighty and Dark Eyes took it to ninety while I paused inside and grew sharp with myself. You've become a desperate and pathetic figure, Amy Dickerson, growing jealous over a stranger's interest in the image of a naked butterball. "Ninety-five to the book," I said.

And there was a brief pause.

I swung back to John Paul. A man like this—how many times had *he* merely seen a woman across a room and he knew he had to get closer to her, had to woo and bed her if he could? Was I suddenly like him? "A hundred? Can you give me a hundred? No way you people are going to let a Renoir go for five figures. You'd be embarrassed to let that happen."

John Paul raised his paddle. "A hundred thousand to John Paul Gibbons."

The bid had run past the order bid in my book and a basic rule for an auctioneer is to play only two bidders at a time. But I didn't want to look at Dark Eyes again. I should have gone back to him, but if he had a thing for this woman who looked so unlike me, then to hell with him, he didn't deserve it. If he was bidding for it—and this thought made me grow warm again—if he was bidding for it merely out of his responsiveness to me, then I didn't want him to waste his money on a second-rate piece. "One ten?" I said and I raised my eyes here on the right side and another paddle went up, about halfway back, a woman who lived on Park Avenue with a house full of Impressionists and a husband twice her age. "One ten to Mrs. Fielding on the right."

She and John Paul moved it up in a few moments to the estimate, one forty. There was another little lull. I said, "It's against you, Mrs. Fielding." Still she hesitated. I should turn to my left, I knew. Dark Eyes could be waiting to give a bid. But instead I went for all the other Mrs. Fieldings. I raised my hand toward the painting, which sat on an easel behind me and to my left. My auctioneer self said, "Doesn't she look like that brief glimpse you had of your dearest aunt at her bath when you were a girl? Or even your dear mama? Her essence is here before you, a great work of art." But the other me, with this left arm lifted, thought—for the first time ever from this podium, because I was always a cool character in this place, always fresh and cool—this other me that had gone quite inexplicably mad thought, My god what if I'm sweating and he's looking at a great dark moon beneath my arm?

I know about desire. It's my job to instill it—blind, irrational desire—in whole crowds of people. But doctors get sick. Lawyers go to jail. Evangelists get caught with prostitutes. There are impulsive attractions that make you feel like you're in control of your life somehow—here's something I want, even superficially, and I'm free to grab it. Then there are the impulsive attractions that only remind you how freedom is a fake. You might be free to *pursue* your desires, but you're never free to *choose* them.

And I had no choice that morning. I lowered my arm abruptly in spite of the fact I hadn't sweat from nerves since I was sixteen. But I'd already made my selling point. I'd stoked the desire of others and Mrs. Fielding took up the pursuit, as did another wealthy woman for a few bids and then another— I played them two at a time—and then it was one of the moneyed women against a little man who dealt in art in the Village and should have known better about this piece, which made me wonder if *he'd* had a life-changing glimpse of his corpulent mama at her bath, but that was the kind of thing my auctioneer self *rightly* ruminated on during the rush of the bidding and I had more or less put Dark Eyes out of my mind and we climbed over a quarter of a million and my boss was beaming in the back of the room and then it stopped, with the little man holding a bid of two hundred and sixty thousand dollars. "It's against you," I said to the woman still in the bidding. She shook her head faintly to say she was out of it.

There is a moment that comes, if you've done your work well, when the whole room finally and abruptly goes, What the hell are we doing? I knew we had reached that moment. But I would have to look back to my left before I could push on to a conclusion.

"Two sixty," I said. "Do I hear two seventy? Two seventy for your sweet Aunt Isabelle? Two sixty then. Fair warning."

Now I looked to him.

His eyes were fixed on me as before and then he smiled, and the unflappable Amy Dickerson, master auctioneer, suddenly flapped. I lost the flow of my words and I stopped. It seemed that he was about to raise his paddle. Don't do it, I thought, trying to send a warning to him across this space. I wrenched my attention away and cried, "Sold! For two hundred and sixty thousand dollars."

I normally use the lull after the gavel, while the lot just sold is taken away and the next one set up, to assess certain buyers that I've learned to read. One woman who sits perfectly still through the bidding for items she has no interest in will suddenly start shuffling her feet when something she wants is about to come up. Another refreshes her lipstick unnecessarily. One distinguished retired surgeon, who always wears a vest, will lift up slightly from where he's sitting, first one cheek and then the other, as if he's passing a perfect pair of farts. But on that morning I was still struggling with an unreasonable obsession. I thought of nothing but this complete stranger and I finally realized that the only way to exorcise this feeling was to confront it, but when at last I worked up the courage to look once more to my left, Dark Eyes had gone.

T hough I'd more or less always competed with her and resented her and criticized her and argued with her and ignored her and heeded her every foolish thought—which is to say I loved her like a sister—Missy and I had lunch once a week in the Village. Sometimes, when we'd grow vaguely irritable with each other for reasons neither of us could put a finger on, one of us would smile a brittle smile at the other and say it just that way. "I love you like a sister," she'd say or I'd say, and then the other would reply, "Just so" or "Me too" or even "Go to hell." And still, we'd tell each other everything, as if there was an actual bond of trust between us, which there was.

So the day after the Crippenhouse auction, over sushi on Thompson Street, I talked about Dark Eyes. "I was relieved," I said, about his vanishing at the end. "But damn if I wasn't wildly disappointed as well."

"So?"

"So? There sat a man like John Paul Gibbons and I'm suddenly acting like his dark twin sister."

"Is John Paul still after you?"

"You're missing the point," I said.

She shrugged. "I don't think so. You're forty now, Amy. You're single. It's hormones and lifestyle."

"Yow," I cried.

"Did you get some wasabi up your nose?"

In fact, I was merely thinking, If you hadn't gone back for your dolls and your clothes I wouldn't be sitting here with you once a week out of familial devotion listening to your complacent hardness of heart. Though I realized, trying to be honest with myself, that my alternative today—and most days—was eating lunch on my own, bolting my food, avoiding the company of men who bored me, a list that got longer every day, it seemed. I resented her stumbling onto a half truth about me and so I leaned toward her and said, "You're thirty-six yourself. You haven't got much longer to be smug."

"That reminds me," Missy said. "Jeff mentioned he saw a poster about that charity auction you're doing in East Hampton."

"How does what I said remind you of that?" I put as much muscle in my voice as I could, but she looked at me as if I'd simply belched. She wasn't going to answer. She had no answer. I knew the answer: her loving husband Jeff the broker was her shield against turning forty. Right. Maybe.

"Mama said she hoped you'd call sometime," Missy said.

I was still following the track under Missy's surface. Mama thought that a beautiful woman like me, as she put it, was either stupid or a lesbian not to have been married by the time I hit forty. And she knew, as God was her witness, that I wasn't a lesbian.

"She hated Daddy by the time she was forty," I said.

"Calm down," Missy said. "Drink some green tea. It's like a sedative."

"And he hated her."

Missy looked away, her mouth tightened into a thin red line.

Okay. I felt guilty for rubbing this in. Both times I'd actually allowed a man to move in with me—all his stuff, no way out, one toilet one life—I eventually arrived at something like hatred for him. In another era, I would have already gone ahead

and married each of them and it would have been no different
for me than for Mama, except she'd never get a divorce.

I followed Missy's eyes across the room. She was looking
at no one, she was just getting pissed with me, but there was
a man leaning across a table for two touching the wrist of the
woman he was with. He was talking quickly, ardently. I looked
away, conscious of my own wrist. Whose gesture was that from
my own life? One of the live-ins. Either Max or Fred. I twisted
my mind away. Who cares which one? I thought. Whoever it
was would say, Amy, Amy, Amy, you get so logical when you're
angry. And yet the touch on my wrist meant he still thought
I was a quaking bundle of nerves beneath the irrefutable points
I'd been making against him. All he had to do was touch me
there and he'd wipe the logic away and prevail. But no way,
Mister. I never lost my logic in an argument, even though
sometimes there were tears, as meaningless as getting wet for
somebody you're just having sex with. I'm crying, I'd say to
him, but don't you dare take it wrong, you son of a bitch. It
was Max.

"I've got to go," my sister said, and I looked at her a little
dazedly, I realized, and we both rose and leaned forward stiffly
from the waist and kissed on the cheek. We split the bill and
my half of the tip was six dollars and twenty-five cents. I watched
her gliding away out the door and then I stared at the money in
my hand.

The Nichols and Gray building is a dreary Fifties thing of concrete and glass on the Upper East Side, as insipid as the old Sotheby's building on Madison, but Arthur Gray won't hear a word against it. "*We're* not the ones who are meant to shine," he says whenever I gripe about the place, always quickly adding, "Except for you, dear. You shine on." Still, it was full of good associations for me, which I found myself very much aware of as I went up in the elevator after my lunch with Missy. So I got off on the second floor just to remind myself what I was all about. I stood in the back doors of the Blue Salon and watched the young men in short-sleeved white shirts and black bow ties, the Lifters and Movers, at the front, setting up the American Art Pottery auction. I looked around at the empty chairs. I could still smell the ardor hovering in the air. Shopping pheromones. They are spoken of in no book, but I know they exist. Those who exude them draw not only other shoppers to them but objects, as well. The young men were laughing. One was wobbling on a ladder setting a spotlight over the stage-left turntable. Even these hormone-besotted boys couldn't get as hot for a piece of ass as some of the pottery-head Central-Park-Westers were going to get when they saw the Shirayamadanis coming to that turntable later in the week.

I slipped out and took the steps up one floor and passed into my outer office without catching anybody's eye. I'd had a quiet morning proofing a big Veteran and Vintage Cars and Motorcycles catalog and even Lydia had been gone for dental work, though she was here now. I could see the shadow of her black tee-shirt beneath her white blouse. She was a Goth leading a double life. Though she'd been with me for nearly three months now, we'd still not spoken a word about any of that. I didn't want to chance putting her off: in her first few days, on her own initiative, she'd brilliantly reorganized my files. In the face of my grateful amazement she simply shrugged and said, "Someday you'll need something real bad and I won't find it and it'll get us both fired." She was a true believer in darkness.

As I whisked past, grabbing the pink called-while-you-were-gone slips, she looked up from her keyboard and furrowed her brow at me. I figured I knew why. She hated filling out these slips, thinking everything should go into my computer. So I waved the slips at her now and said, "Computers crash."

"That's not the issue," she said.

"What, then?"

"Am I free to speak?"

"I won't fire you for speaking your mind. You know that."

"Okay. What's with the Frenchmen?"

"What Frenchmen?"

"Christie's got bought. Phillips got bought. By two different French guys. Now Mr. Gray's burning up the lines to Paris like it's phone-sex."

"You're afraid the French are going to buy Nichols and Gray and they'll fire us both?"

Lydia shrugged.

Arthur's Paris calls were indeed news to me. There were other explanations, of course. But it was also like Arthur Gray to keep me out of the business loop until the last minute. "Lydia, they need me here. I need you. We're safe."

Lydia sighed and she stared hard at me, I think to stop herself from rolling her eyes in contempt.

I said, "You think I'm blind to the dark forces of the universe."

This surprised her. But she reflected no more than a nano-second on my insight before she leaped ahead a few steps in a presumed conversation that kept me comfortably ignorant of her. "Okay, Ms. Dickerson. I'll chill."

It's not where I was going, but I didn't bother to dispute her. "Good," I said, and I went into my office and sat down and I waited long enough so it wouldn't seem as if I was going off to check on what Lydia had said and then I went off to check on what Lydia had said.

Arthur's secretary had her back to me—a long dark drape of hair. I could see her and Lydia done up in black PVC in some club on the Lower East Side comparing notes on their bosses uptown. But I kept my mouth shut. For one thing, I wanted to keep my pipeline open to Arthur's office.

"Hi, Winona," I said to her and before she could turn I barged on into Arthur's office, as was my custom.

WQXR was playing low in the background—some simpering generic baroque thing—and Arthur was on the phone. He blew me a kiss with his fingertips and motioned me to a chair.

"Of course," he said into the phone. "Mais oui." At the French phrase—which he pronounced beautifully, though I knew it to be one of only perhaps a dozen that he knew—he winked at me. Arthur could be vain over odd little things, like his perfect pronunciation of a language he didn't speak, but this time I took the wink as a reflection of his guilty conscience. I arrived at just the right moment. "I'll see you next week," he said to Paris. "Au revoir. And bon voyage."

Heady with three killer phrases in a row, Arthur hung up and squared around to me. "Amy, my hero. You were magnificent last night."

I said, "Elle a eu son heure de gloire."

Arthur frowned. "Now, my dear, you know I can't speak a word of that language."

"He'd never guess," I said, nodding to the phone.

"Ah. Well. I think he knows."

Suddenly it occurred to me that the Gothnet had leaped to the wrong conclusion. Arthur simply had a new boyfriend.

This seemed even more likely as he veered back to the auction. "That might well be the worst Renoir I've ever seen. To sell that for what you did, my dear, was pure genius." He slicked a hand back over his hair, which he'd abruptly died chestnut—the color of his youth, he said—the day after he turned sixty. I grew suspicious again.

"Arthur, is it time to tell me something?"

"Of course, my dear. I was just waiting for Alain to arrive in town so we three could sit down together."

"Alain?"

Arthur nodded solemnly at the phone. "Alain Bouchard."

"So we do have a French suitor?"

"We do. Ours is the best of the lot, too."

"Arthur, the secretaries all know already."

"He's racehorses and wine and Mirage jets, or at least some crucial part of them."

"Arthur," I said sharply. "Pay attention."

He blinked and focused on me.

I said, "You've called me 'my dear' twice in a minute and a half. You know you've done something wrong."

"And 'my hero,' too," he admitted, hanging his head.

"There. You see?"

"The secretaries know?"

"Yes they do. I don't."

"I'm sorry, Amy. You understand it's not from lack of respect for you. I didn't think anybody on this side of the Atlantic knew but me and Pookie's ghost." Arthur crossed himself, which was rather like his speaking French. He wasn't Catholic, or even religious. Pookie had been Philip Nichols, the Nichols of Nichols and Gray.

I waited. Arthur meditated. I presumed on his dear departed Pookie. Then he said, "Two hundred and sixty thousand dollars for that bloody awful painting. You outdid yourself."

"Arthur, now you're starting to sound British. That's the next stage when you're feeling guilty. I suppose I know what that's about."

"No you don't. I'm doing everything I can."

"You promised me a chance to buy in some day."

"Alain knows what an asset you are in all this. I told him he had to give you a piece of it. Stock or something. He's got plenty of stock."

"And?"

"He's anxious to meet you."

"That has the whiff of euphemism," I said.

"The whiff's not coming from me," Arthur said. I waited for a hand to fly up to smooth his hair, but both of them stayed on the desktop. Furthermore, he was looking at me unwaveringly in the eyes. In short, I believed him.

But it was also clear I'd gotten as much as I was going to get out of Arthur for now and I rose from the chair. "I'd tell you to watch out for what your secretary's hearing," I said, "but that may be the only way I'll ever find out what's going on."

Now one of Arthur's hands rose from the desk, hovered for a moment, and then did a one-eighty flip, a presto-changeo gesture. "Here now, my dear," he said. "A fun thing. An apartment on Central Park West chockablock full of Victoriana, all for us. Monday you get to go play."

The thing he wanted to changeo was my mood. Arthur hated seeing me unhappy. The sad thing was, this worked.

The auction business is built on the three "d's": debt, divorce, and death. Monday morning I entered a russet brick and terra-cotta apartment building where a reclusive woman who loved her Victoriana had died in her sleep six weeks ago. I was not unaware that the quickening in me— yes, the happiness—over the prospect of eight rooms of stuff to handle and ponder and classify and value was directly a result of a woman's death. Her only son would meet me, so I squelched my pleasure and chose from one of three Nichols-and-Gray first-meeting demeanors—the debt counselor or the divorce attorney or the mortician. I was least comfortable with the latter, but that was the obvious choice.

The doorman had my name and I went up in an elevator that smelled faintly of Obsession and I rang the bell at the woman's apartment. And when the door swung open I found myself standing before Dark Eyes.

I'm sure I let the creature beneath the mortician—indeed, even beneath the gleefully object-obsessed auctioneer—show her face in that moment: the little half smile that came over Dark Eyes told me so. The smile was faintly patronizing, as well. But I forgave him that. I was, after all, making myself a gawking fool at the moment. The smile also suggested, I realized, that he had requested me specifically for this evaluation. I focused on that thought, even as I reasserted my professionalism.

"I'm Amy Dickerson," I said. "Of Nichols and Gray."

He bowed faintly and he repeated my name. "Ms. Dickerson." He was a little older than I thought, from close up, and even handsomer. His cheekbones were high and his eyes were darker than I'd been able to see from the podium. "I'm Trevor Martin. Mrs. Edward Martin's son."

"I'm glad," I said, and to myself I said, What the hell does that mean? "To meet you," I added, though I fooled neither of us. I was glad he was here and I was here. The only thing I wasn't glad about was that his name was Trevor. It was a name made for a rainy climate and bowler hats.

"Come in," he said and I did and I nearly staggered from the Victorian profusion of the place. The foyer was stuffed full: an umbrella stand and a grandfather clock and a stand-up coat-rack and a dozen dark-framed hunting scenes and a giltwood and gesso mirror and a Gothic-style cupboard and a papier-mâché prie-dieu with shell-inlaid cherubs and a top-rail of red velvet, and Trevor—I had to think of him as that now, at least till I could call him Dark Eyes to his face—Trevor was moving ahead of me

and I followed him into Mrs. Edward Martin's parlor—and my
eyes could not hold still, there was such a welter of things, and I
went from fainting bench to pump organ to the William Morris
Strawberry Thief wallpaper—the walls were aswirl with vines and
flowers and strawberries and speckled birds.

"I don't know where the smell of lilacs is coming from,"
he said.

I looked at him, not prepared for that cognitive leap. I
looked back to a mantelpiece filled with parian porcelains of
Shakespeare, General Gordon, Julius Caesar, Victoria herself
threatening to fall from the edge where she'd been jostled by
the crowd of other white busts.

"It's always in my clothes after I visit here."

"What's that?" I said, trying to gain control of my senses.

"The lilac. I never asked her where it came from, but now
when I'm free to look, I can't find it."

"You must miss her," I said.

"Is that what I'm conveying?" His voice had gone flat.

I didn't even know myself why I'd jumped to that conclusion, much less expressed it. Maybe it was all her stuff around
me. See me, love me, miss me, she was crying, I am so intricate
and so ornamented that you can't help but do that. But Trevor
clearly had seen her, and whether or not he'd loved her, I don't
think he missed her much. Evidently he heard his own tone,
because he smiled at me and he made his voice go so soft from
what seemed like self-reflection that my hands grew itchy to
touch him. "That must sound like an odd response," he said.
"How could an only child not miss his mother?"

"I can think of ways."

He smiled again but this time at the room. He looked around. "Do you wonder if I grew up amidst all this?"

"Yes."

"I did."

"And you want to get rid of it."

His smile came back to me. He looked at me closely and he was no Trevor at all. "Every bit," he said.

That first day, I sat at a bentwood table in the kitchen and he would bring me the things he could carry—a sterling silver biscuit box and a cut glass decanter, a coach-lace coffee cozy and a silver and gold peacock pendant, and on and on—and I would make notes for the catalog description and I would give him an estimate and he never challenged a figure, never asked a question. At some point I realized it was past two and we ordered in Chinese and he had already rolled the sleeves on his pale green silk shirt and we ate together, me using chopsticks, him using a fork. In the center of the table sat a spring-driven tabletop horse-racing toy with eight painted lead horses with jockeys that circled a grooved wooden track. He had just put it before me when the doorbell rang with the food.

We ate in silence for a couple of minutes, a nice silence, I thought—we were comfortable enough with each other already that we didn't have to make small talk. Finally, though, I pointed to the toy and asked, "Was this yours?"

"Not really. It was around. I never played with it."

"Weren't you allowed?"

"How much will we get?" he said.

"Toys aren't a specialty of mine. I can only get you into the ballpark."

"Close enough."

"I think the estimate would be around three hundred dollars."

"And you'd work the bid up to six."

I looked at the row of jockeys. "Probably a little more. Understand that estimates usually run low. To whet appetites. And we do have a couple of regulars who play the horses. And more than a couple are still kids at heart."

"You're scary sometimes, Amy Dickerson, what you can pick up in people." He was smiling the same smile I'd taken for self-reflection.

"This might be true," I said. I was up to my elbows here in mothers and children and my own mother thought the same thing about me, expecting all the good men in the world to be frightened away. Looking into Trevor's dark eyes I felt a twist of something in my chest that the cool and collected part of me recognized as panic.

"I mean that in an admiring way," he said.

"How come I didn't pick up on that?"

"I'm sorry. I scare people, too."

"But you don't scare me. See the problem I'm suddenly faced with? We have an imbalance here."

"In the courtroom," he said.

"You're a lawyer?"

"Yes."

"That *is* scary," I said, and part of me meant it.

"I only defend the poor and the downtrodden," he said.

"Not if you can afford silk shirts."

"That was two categories. I defend the poor and the down-trodden rich."

"Is there such a thing?"

"Ask any rich man. He'll tell you."

"What about rich women?"

The playfulness drained out of him, pulling the corners of his mouth down. I knew he was thinking about his mother again.

"Trevor," I said, softly. He looked me in the eyes and I said, "Play the game."

For a moment he didn't understand.

I nodded to the spring-driven tabletop horse-racing toy with eight hollowcast, painted lead horses with jockeys and grooved wooden track, estimate three hundred dollars. He followed my gesture and looked at the object for a moment. Then he stretched and pulled it to him and he put his hand on the key at the side. He hesitated and looked at me. Ever so slightly I nodded, yes.

He turned the key and the kitchen filled with the metallic scrinch of the gears and he turned it again and again until it would turn no more. Then he tripped the release lever and the horses set out jerking around the track once, twice, a horse taking the lead and then losing it to another and that one losing it to another until the sound ceased and the horses stopped. Trevor's eyes had never left the game. Now he looked at me.

"Which one was yours?" I asked.

He reached out his hand and laid it over mine. Our first touch. "They all were," he said.

There was a time when I thought I would be a model. I *was* a model. I did the catwalk glide as well as any of them, selling the clothes, selling the attitude. And off the job—when I was in my own jeans and going, Who the hell was I today?—I had trouble figuring out how to put one foot in front of the other one without feeling like I was still on the runway. There was a time when I was an actress. I was Miss Firecracker and I was Marilyn Monroe and I was passionate about a shampoo and I was still going, Who the hell was I today? Then there were the two live-ins. They didn't help ease Mama's angst. People actually think to get married, in Texas, she'd observe. It didn't help ease my angst either. I was "Babe" to one and "A.D." to the other and one never made a sound when we had sex and the other yelled, "Oh Mama," over and over, and I found part of myself sitting somewhere on the other side of the room watching all this and turning over the same basic question.

So what was I reading in Trevor Martin, the once and perhaps future Dark Eyes, that would make me hopeful? After he put his hand on mine he said, "I've been divorced for six months. My mother has been dead for six weeks. It feels good to have a woman look inside me. That's not really happened before. But I'm trying to move slowly into the rest of my life."

"I understand," I said, and I did. "For one thing, we have every object of your childhood to go through first."

He squeezed my hand gently, which told me he'd known I'd understand and he was grateful.

I left him on the first evening and went to a Thai restaurant and ate alone, as had been my recent custom, though I felt the possibilities with Dark Eyes unfurling before me. But that didn't stop me from eating too fast and I walked out with my brow sweating and my lips tingling from the peppers.

And I went home to my apartment and I stepped in and when I switched on the lights, I was stopped cold. My eyes leaped from overstuffed chair to overstuffed couch to silk Persian rug and all of it was in fin de siècle Bloomingdale's earth tones and it was me, it was what was left of me after I'd been dead for six weeks and somebody that wasn't me but was *like* me was here to catalog it all and there was a ficus in a corner and a signed Dalí print of the Virgin Mary and her baby over the empty mantelpiece and a wall of bookshelves and I wanted to turn around and walk out, go to a bar or back to work, take my notes from the first day at Mrs. Edward Martin's and go put them in a computer, anything but step further into this apartment with its silence buzzing in my ears.

Then I saw the red light flashing on my answering machine and I moved into my apartment as if nothing odd was going on. I approached the phone, which sat, I was suddenly acutely aware, on an Angelo Donghia maple side table with Deco-style tapering legs, estimated value eight hundred dollars. But the flashing light finally cleared my head: I had one message and I pushed the button.

It was Arthur Gray. "Hello, Amy," he said. "I'm so sorry about yesterday. I promise to tell you about my every move from now on." At this, Arthur laughed a little hee-hee laugh. "Professional move, that is. I hope you had fun today with all the bric-a-brac. I forgot to mention the benefit auction. Woody Allen just came through with a walk-on part in his new film. *Postmodern Millie,* I think it's going to be called. And the mayor's offered a dinner at Gracie Mansion. But I've had a special request, and since we're not being *entirely* altruistic here—rightly not—I really think we should do it. More later. You know how I appreciate you. Our best customers are your biggest admirers . . . Almost forgot. Do you need a lift to the Hamptons Saturday? We should get out there early and I've got a limo. Let me know. Bye."

All of which barely registered at the time. I realized it was the assumption that the red light was Trevor that had cleared the mortality from my head.

On that night I sat naked on the edge of my bed, my silk nightshirt laid out beside me, and I thought of Trevor, the silk of his shirt the color of a ripe honeydew, or the color—if green is the color of jealousy—of the pallid twinge I felt when I found Max, in the third year of our relationship, in a restaurant we'd been to together half a dozen times, only this time he had a woman hanging on his arm. He saw me. I saw him. It was lunchtime and I sat down at a table, my back to him, and I ate my lunch alone, which I'd planned to do, and very fast, faster than usual. I loved that Caesar salad and split pea soup, in spite of the speed, perhaps because of it: I was furious. Only the tiniest bit jealous, surprisingly, but angry. I love to eat when I'm angry. He wouldn't talk about it that night. The one on his arm never argued with him, he said. She was just about as stupid and irrational as he himself was, he said, thinking, I suppose, that he was being ironic. But even at that moment I thought it was the first truthful thing he'd said in a long time.

I laid my hand on the nightshirt. The silk was cool and slick and I clenched it with my fingers like a lover's back. And then I let it go. It was Fred's shirt. It had been too big for pasty slender Fred. I looked at it. Periwinkle blue. White oyster buttons. Soft tip collar. Versace. Two hundred and fifty dollars. Who'll start the bidding at nothing? I looked at the shirt and wondered why I hadn't given it away or thrown it away from the negative provenance. But I didn't give a damn about that. It felt good to sleep in. That was a healthy attitude, surely.

I looked around the room. And my eyes moved to my dresser and found a silver tankard stuffed with an arrangement of dried flowers. I rose and crossed to it and picked it up. It was from Max. The tankard, not the flowers. It was Georgian with a baluster shape and a flared circular foot and a light engraved pattern of flowers and foliate scrolls. He'd been an ignorant gift-giver. Magazine subscriptions and sweaters. I vaguely remembered challenging him about it and he'd bought me this for seven hundred dollars. On eBay, where every grandma and pack rat is her own auction house. And he'd gotten me a glorified beer mug. But I was grateful at the time. He wanted to use it himself, I realized. He said the silver was the only thing that would keep a beer cold in the Georgian era. Yum, he said. But I didn't let him use it even once. I put flowers in his beer mug and I kept it to this moment, standing naked and alone in my bedroom, my face twisted beyond recognition in the reflection in my hand. It was beautiful, this object, really. That's why I kept it. Both these men had vanished forever from this place. Exorcised. The objects they touched—a thing I would push like crazy in an auction if they'd been famous and dead—held not a trace of them. And I felt the chilly creep of panic in my limbs at this thought.

I put the tankard down and turned away. I crossed to the bed and I lifted this Versace shirt with soft tip collar and I let it fall over my head and down, the silk shimmering against me, and suddenly I felt as if I'd climbed inside Trevor's skin. Can you trust to know a man from a pair of dark eyes? From Chinese food and a child's game played by an adult after a lifetime of quiet pain inflicted by a mother? From the touch of a hand? Inside this draping of silk my body had its own kind of logic. These details *are* the man, my body reasoned, as surely as the buttons and the stitching and the weave of cloth are this two-hundred-and-fifty-dollar shirt. I raised my paddle and I bid on this man.

"One thousand dollars," I said.

Auctioneers are attuned to a certain gesture that is not a gesture, to the sudden presence of a thing that has no presence. I'm speaking of the *hesitation*. I sensed it in Trevor. We had before us on the kitchen bentwood table a sterling silver Edward Barnard and Sons centerpiece in squared oval-form on four appliqué legs and the room had been bright with sunlight all morning and it surely had made my finely textured, newly light-ash-blond hair diaphanously beautiful and I handled these objects of his mother's life with great tenderness, and yet for the whole of this morning Trevor had been all business. Which is probably why I had just given him an estimate half of what it probably should have been—even factoring in that estimates usually run low. As a little test. This is not a good quality in me, I suppose. But yesterday he laid his hand on mine and today he had not even brushed past my shoulder on his way into the other room to gather up more objects. And he seemed way too focused, in this process, on the Money Moment. Now granted, that is a thing I should hardly be criticizing in a client, especially one who no doubt had legitimate issues with the dead collector of these objects. But here I was alone with him all morning and he'd backslid seriously and so I pushed this little needle into him.

I let his hesitation play on for a moment and then I asked, "Is there something wrong?"

"No," he said, not moving his eyes from the centerpiece.

"The money…"

"It's not that," he said quickly, even ardently, and he looked at me.

I was relieved to find I believed him, though now, from guilt, my mind wouldn't get off the money. "I don't mean it as the estimate," I said. "A thousand would be more like the opening bid."

"Look," he said, nodding to the centerpiece. I did.

"I have trouble seeing the world like that," he said.

I knew what he meant: the body of the piece was profuse with chased flowers and leaves and fruit baskets and each leg held the face of a child nearly smothered in ruffles and scrolls.

"It's *all* like that," he said.

I wished I could say, You're going to like my apartment. I couldn't, but at least I was feeling again it might come to that. Which meant more guilt, me thinking about romance while he was struggling to come to terms with the mother with each object we examined. So this time I laid my hand on his.

And before even I could figure out what my primary intent was, the phone rang.

I lifted my hand at once. Trevor rose and went to the wall phone by the door and answered. I let his voice turn into a murmur and I looked out the window to the treetops of Central Park. I found myself not wanting to know who might call him. I refused to let this headlong silliness that was going on inside me include jealousy. I concentrated on the park, thinking, who are we trying to kid with all these trees? This is goddam New York City. Get used to it.

"It's for you," Trevor said.

I almost said, "Good." But I clamped my mouth shut and rose and took the phone.

It could only be Arthur. He said, "Hello, my dear. Mr. Martin has kindly agreed to give you a few hours off. He's here and we're to have lunch."

"He?"

"Alain Bouchard. Come twinkle."

"Where?"

"You won't believe it."

Down the block from the Nichols and Gray building is the Provenance Deli, the place we all go or send out to for lunch, with sandwiches named The Chippendale and The Tiffany and The Art Deco and all of it straight New York Deli, the Deco, for example, being square-cut turkey, triangle-cut salami, and halved cherry tomatoes. I moved through the packed-too-close marble-top tables full of lunchers to the back of the place where Arthur's table sat in a corner beneath some third-rate Victorian landscapes the deli owner had picked up cheap at one of our arcade sales. Arthur rose at my approach, and also rising, beside him, more slowly, was a tall, broad-set, early fifty-something man—perhaps even a vigorously preserved late-fifties—with a tanned, smooth-molded face and nearly black eyes and tightly cropped hair faintly graying at the edges. It was a face from a black-and-white film with subtitles and probably costarring Jeanne Moreau. His hands were large, too, as both of them took mine. I'd offered a simple handshake but was instead being engulfed by hands that were smooth to the touch but felt as hard as the hands of, say, a Marseilles dockworker.

Arthur was making introductions that I ignored and Alain Bouchard and I looked at each other directly and we did not so much as blink. For a long moment I concentrated on standing up to a possible future boss and he concentrated, I assumed, on being the guy with the dough and the clout. Then he said, "I've heard so much about you."

He spoke with only the faintest trace of an accent, just a little pinchy thing around some of the vowels. "I've heard almost nothing about you," I said.

Alain glanced sharply at Arthur who beamed at each of us in turn. Alain turned his eyes back to me. "I will have to explain myself," he said and he motioned us both to our chairs. "Please."

He waited where he stood for us to settle in and then he waited another few beats, him towering above the two of us. It was a cheap trick, this little tableau of power, and I refused to raise my eyes to him.

Arthur, however, toggled obsequiously between Alain and me. I wanted to kick him under the table to make him stop, but instead, with my eyes fixed on my sweet-natured, pathetic, antique-maven of a boss, I said, "First Arthur has to explain why he's brought you to *this* place for lunch."

"That is an easy thing," Alain said, finally descending. "I insisted. His first suggestion was a French restaurant. I said to him, 'How absurd, isn't it? I have too many French lunches. I am from France. I come to New York, so I wish to go to a New York deli.'"

Arthur forced a little laugh. "I tried to carry coals to Newcastle."

I looked at Alain. He was puzzling this out, I realized. I

said, "You're trying to understand how you've become a lump of coal."

Alain laughed. "I still treat an unfamiliar idiom as a mathematical equation to work out the x and the y. But now I see. Porter de l'eau à la rivière. Am I right?" He turned to Arthur as if he understood the French. I could not tell if Arthur's little pretense of knowing the language had betrayed him now for the first time or if Alain was needling Arthur for something that had already come out between them.

Either way, I felt bad for Arthur and jumped in. "To carry water to the river," I said.

"Yes," Alain said. "Good. This is the thing we have avoided." Then he made a show of opening the menu. "So tell me why the Louis XIV sandwich is made of sun-dried tomatoes, chopped liver, and Swiss cheese."

"The owner hates the French," I said.

Alain nodded sedately at this, without looking up from the menu.

It was Arthur who jumped in now, clearly thinking he'd help me out of what he took to be an embarrassing situation. He said, "All in good fun. They did a sandwich of me once. Roast beef, tongue, and American cheese. And they like me."

Alain laughed and squinted hard at the menu. "Where is this Arthur Gray sandwich? That is what I will have. With Dijon mustard."

"I'm afraid you won't find me there. They took it off some time ago. I was a slow seller."

"Ah but they have made a mistake," Alain said. "That is a very fine combination."

Arthur brushed aside the remark with a wave of the hand as if it were complimentary to him. "They're working on an Amy Dickerson, I'm told."

This was the first I'd heard of it and probably a lie. But Alain put down his menu and said, "How wonderful. And Mademoiselle Dickerson, what would you like to see on your sandwich?"

"Testicules du taureau," I said. "Plain."

Alain finally flinched. Then he threw his head back and laughed. I felt a little better about Alain for this, though I knew I was still on Arthur's side. It occurred to me that Arthur had missed the operative word in my sandwich meat, given the French pronunciation. I turned to him and he was looking a little blank. I leaned to him. "Prairie oysters," I said, though my daddy's name for them left Arthur just as baffled. It pleased me now to say it bluntly, for both of these men. "Bull's balls," I said.

I once auctioned a jar of them. A large jar, specially prepared and preserved, sold with a rich catalog of other culinary curiosities from the effects of a great Spanish cook who'd run a Valencian restaurant on the Upper East Side and died from a heart attack with his face buried in a paella. I sold these criadillas for nearly three thousand dollars. Someone cared passionately about that jar of bull's balls. I had coaxed out that passion, led it along to the moment when he possessed this thing. And on the afternoon of this first lunch, after small talk and our sandwiches—Alain finally special-ordered roast beef, tongue, and American cheese with Dijon mustard—and as we drank our coffee, Alain did at last explain himself and I decided he would understand the man who bought that jar. "I adore the collector," he said. "I adore the collecting spirit. The man or the woman who loves to collect is a man or woman who loves the rich variety of life. We can only live among things. Even the monks, who are supposed to own nothing, had their stones and their beads and their sandals and the bright illumination of words that flowed from their quill pens. They surely held this quill pen or that quill pen and appreciated what could be wrought with it. The object itself was wonderful to them. No one can ignore objects, and the collector says, Yes. Yes, I will embrace these things. I will treasure these things. I will own these things so that I might possess a little of what the world is all about. It is like identity, is it not? I own this thing, therefore I am? I am making a partial jest now. But only partial. We choose the objects around us to discover who we are. Don't you agree?"

I felt a little breathless. In spite of there being a faint air of bullshit about this rush of words. Wasn't all this sounding a little like the flow of rhetoric from an articulate seducer who, at the end of the day, only wants to fuck you? But I was breathless nonetheless. "I agree," I said.

"Oh yes," said Arthur, who was ready to be seduced.

Alain nodded approvingly at us both.

I had a thought about what he'd just said—that for some it's more, I *buy,* therefore I am. In spite of my suspicions about him, I liked his provoking this kind of meditation on what we do. But I figured this man who might soon be my boss wanted to hear only his own words right now, so I kept my mouth shut.

He said, "Then for me to buy Nichols and Gray, this is a very postmodern thing, is it not?"

I think we both showed a blankness at this turn in his ideas, a moment I suspect he relished in and of itself. He was in control. He let us dangle, and then he said, "At least the part of postmodernism that in a writer, for instance, might make him create a work about creating a work. Metafiction, you call it? Unlike my other businesses—which I collect, I make no secret of that element in what I do—with Nichols and Gray I am collecting a thing whose very existence is about collecting things. Do you understand?"

"This is your metabusiness," Arthur said.

Alain was pleased. "Exactly."

"So you should not be so concerned about our profit and loss," Arthur said. Our balance sheet—which had suffered with the stock market—must have been an important price-setting point in the discussions so far. For all his dithering and occasional pretense, Arthur was still a shrewd cookie. Now it was Alain who was caught off guard.

It didn't last long. Alain cocked his head at Arthur and smiled a pouty smile and I thought of Maurice Chevalier about to do a dance step. He said, "If you find even one more buyer who will desire you for the same thing, perhaps. But I am the exception. The eccentric. The world at large has its own standards. And there, you have an appropriate value. We all do, do we not?"

With this, Alain turned his smile to me, as well. I looked away.

If Alain Bouchard did nothing else, he got me to thinking anew about fundamentals. How *do* you assess the value of a thing? People in the business talk about this and that, but it comes down to five major objective standards. The condition: the more nearly perfect, the better. The rarity: the rarer, the better. The size: usually neither too big nor too small. The provenance: not just the record of ownership but the personal history of the object, the more extraordinary—either good or bad—the better. The authenticity: though a fake may be, to any but an informed eye, indistinguishable from the true object, the world of the auction will cast out the pretender.

After lunch I went to the corner and took out my cell phone while the two men walked back toward Nichols and Gray. I watched them, Alain quite tall and wide-shouldered, Arthur narrow and diminutive, fully a head shorter. One seemed too big, the other too small, but both struck me as unquestionably rare. Deep down, how authentic either one of them was, was still an open question.

I called Trevor's apartment on my cell phone. He picked up and said at once, "Hello, Amy."

I was stopped by this. "My cell phone doesn't register on caller ID," I said.

"It could be no one but you at this moment," he said.

I felt very odd about that response for reasons that weren't apparent to me. I squinted into the street, looking at nothing in particular for a few beats, trying unsuccessfully to figure this out.

"You're finished with your lunch," Trevor said.

"Yes."

"Will you come back this afternoon?" he said. There was something almost plaintive in his voice.

"Yes," I said.

And nothing happened. We sat side by side. We handled and pondered and evaluated object after object. And he did not so much as brush my arm passing by, though the warmth stayed in his eyes and in his voice. I was weary of feeling caught off guard with men. I reminded myself that this was a man dealing with the death of his mother. Dealing with the rest of his life. Blah blah blah. And so I focused on my work and I turned off the spigot of my own pheromones. Wrench tight.

And then it was Friday, our fifth and final day of assessments in the apartment of the deceased Mrs. Edward Martin, mother of Trevor Martin. On this fifth day he opened the door to my ringing the bell and this fifth silk shirt he wore was bloused in the sleeves and open to the third button and his chest was covered with dark down and his smile was so deeply appreciative of my standing there waiting to be let in that I thought for a moment he was about to take me in his arms and kiss me. And I was no longer in control of my attitude. Fuck the spigot, I didn't even have the option of turning it back on or not, the goddam pipe burst and I was suddenly up to my nostrils in my own ardor. I was more than ready for him to make a move.

But he did not. Nor did I, I suppose from a residue of Texas mores still in me, which I didn't like. But I wasn't compelled to override them and he obviously had another agenda, and so we spent the morning and the first hours of the afternoon working our way around the larger pieces in the foyer, the parlor, the library, the dining room. Then after I'd assessed a beautiful mahogany three-pedestal dining table with brass paw feet, he said, "You're hungry." He was right. And for the second day in a row he did not even ask what I wanted but went to the phone and ordered my favorite Chinese dishes—though, in all honesty, I would have varied my fare if he'd asked—but I found myself liking his presumption, liking that he should know this domestic detail about me.

And after we ate, he took me to a small room lined completely with armoires in rosewood and mahogany and walnut, and filling the armoires were all things that could be embroidered—quilts and drapes and cushions and bellows and doilies and on and on, big things and small—and there were Persian rugs stacked knee high in the center of the floor and on top of them sat two open steamer trunks, overflowing with indistinguishable cloth objects all frilled and flowered.

"I'm surprised at her," I said without thinking. "She's out of control in here."

"This was my room," Trevor said.

I turned to him, wanting to take the words back.

"It didn't look like this," he said, smiling.

I had a strong impulse now to lean forward and lay my forehead against the triangle of his exposed chest. But I held still. I would not push him into the rest of his life. Then he said, "Let's leave this room for later," and he was moving away. I followed him down the hallway and he paused at a closed door, the only room I hadn't seen. He hesitated, not looking at me, but staring at the door itself as if trying to listen for something on the other side. I quickly sorted out the apartment in my head and I realized that this must have been her bedroom.

How long had it been since I'd made love? Some months. Too many months. One of the great, largely unacknowledged jokes Nature plays on women—at least this woman—is to increase one's desire for sex while decreasing one's tolerance for boring men. Horny and discriminating is a bad combination, it seems to me. And the situation before me—exceedingly strange though it was shaping up to be—was anything but boring. Still he hesitated.

I said, "This is hard for you."

He nodded.

He opened the door and I had no choice but to step to his side and look in.

There were probably some pots and pans, a telephone and a commode, some kitchen utensils, that were not Victorian in Mrs. Edward Martin's apartment. But almost nothing else. Except now I was looking at her bed and it was eighteenth-century Italian with a great arched headboard painted pale blue and parcel-gilt-carved with lunettes, and rising at each side was a pale pink pilaster topped not by a finial but by a golden cupid, his bow and arrow aimed at the bed. The smell of lilacs rolled palpably from the room, Trevor put his arm around my shoulders, and some little voice in my head was going, How desperate have you become?

Then he gave me a quick friendly squeeze and his arm disappeared from around me and he said, "Maybe I'll let you do this room on your own."

"Right," I said, and I sounded as if I was choking.

An hour later I found him sitting at the kitchen table, sipping a cup of coffee. I sat down across from him. We were quiet together for a time, and finally he said, "Do you want some coffee?"

"No," I said. "Thanks."

He stared into his own cup for a long moment and then he said, "She loved objects."

"That's clear."

"My childhood, her adulthood. It was all one," he said softly. "She had a good eye. She knew what she wanted and she knew what it would cost and she was ready to pay it."

He was saying these things with a tone that sounded like tenderness. On our first evening he'd taken pleasure in my being able to look inside him, but at this moment he seemed opaque. He felt tender about her shopping? But then it made a kind of sense. I, of all people, should understand his mother. I played people like her every day.

I made my voice go gentle, matching his tone. "What she saw and loved and bought, this was how she said who she was." And a little chill suddenly ran through me. This had been Alain's point, I realized.

Trevor looked at me and nodded faintly. "Like style. We

are what we wear. We are what we hang on our walls. Perhaps you're right. She was talking to me."

He looked away.

And I thought: the buying isn't the point; it's that we *under-stand* the objects. We love what we understand. And then I averted my eyes from the next logical step. But I can see it now, replaying it all: we love what we understand, and there I sat, understanding Trevor Martin.

I waited for him to say more but he seemed content with the silence. I was not. I was doing entirely too much thinking. I said, "I've solved your mystery."

He smiled at me and cocked his head. The smile was reassuring. It was okay to move on.

I said, "Her pillows—and there were a dozen of them—they all had lilac sachets stuffed inside the cases."

"Of course. I should have realized. She slept in it."

I found I was relieved that even in his freedom to search for the source of the scent he had avoided her bedclothes. And he had not made love to me on her bed. These were good and reassuring things. I was free now to relax with my pleasure in the way he lifted his eyebrows each time he sipped his coffee, the way he lifted his chin to enjoy the taste, the way his eyes moved to the right and his mouth bunched up slightly when he grew thoughtful, the way—for the second time—he reached out and laid his hand on mine. I was filled with the details of him. I could sell him for a million bucks. Not that I would. Clearly, part of me was beginning to think he was a keeper.

When his hand settled on my hand, he said, "I will sleep better tonight because of you."

I looked at him with a little stutter in my chest. I'd suddenly become what my daddy used to call "cow-simple." It was from his touch. It was from merely the word "sleeping." It was stupid but I was having trouble figuring out what he was really trying to say.

And he let me gape on, as if I was out alone in a field, paused in the middle of chewing my cud, wondering where I was. Then he said, "The mystery. Solved."

"Of course," I said.

When this fifth workday was done, for the fifth time he walked me to the door and thanked me, rather formally, for all that I was doing. Tonight I stopped and looked into his eyes when he said this. "I've enjoyed your company," I said.

"And I've enjoyed yours," he said.

That's all I wanted to say. I turned to go.

"Amy," he said.

I turned back and my instinct said this was the time he would take me into his arms. My instinct was wrong. Was this another trend for the forty-year-old woman? Horny, discriminating, and utterly without sexual intuition? He simply said, "I'll see you down."

We went out the door together and along the hall and I pushed the down button on the elevator and a spark of static electricity bit at my fingertip. That was it, I thought. I've now discharged into the electrical system of the building elevators whatever it was I was feeling a few moments ago.

The doors opened. We stepped in. The doors closed. We were alone, and maybe the elevators did suck up the charge that was between us, because we descended one floor of the ten we had to go and Trevor reached out and flipped the red switch on the panel and the elevator bounced to a stop and a bell began ringing and he took me in his arms and I leaped up and hooked my legs around him as we kissed. He pressed me against the wall and he did not make a sound.

The next day I leaned into the tinted window of Arthur Gray's limo and faced the rush of trees and light standards and, eventually, industrial parks, along the Long Island Expressway. I never had understood what men saw in lovemaking in a standing position. Though Trevor had been strong enough, certainly, to hold me up without my constantly feeling like I would slip off him. He was silent, but he did not cry out, Oh Mama, which would have been much worse, under the circumstances. We'd not had a proper date. We'd never even gone out for a meal. But that sounded like my Mama talking. I was well-fucked and unusually meditative.

When we were on Highway 27, out among the potato fields and vegetable stands and runs of quaint shops and approaching East Hampton, Arthur finally roused me from going nowhere in my head. He said, "Amy, there's one more item that I want you to put on your list. Okay?"

"Okay."

"It's the special request I mentioned on your machine."

Arthur was shuffling his feet and talking all around something and he'd finally gotten me interested, even suspicious.

"What are you talking about, Arthur?"

"A dinner with you."

"With me?"

"At Fellini's. In Soho. They've already donated the meal, with wine. Dinner for two with the most beautiful auctioneer in New York."

I was silent. This was really troubling for a reason I couldn't quite define.

"Come on," he said. "Think of the whales."

"This is for whales? I thought it was for a disease."

"Whales get diseases, too. The point is that your mystique, which is considerable, is Nichols and Gray's mystique, as well. Give somebody a dandy candlelit dinner. For us. Okay?"

There was no good reason to say no. I liked whales. I liked Arthur. I liked Nichols and Gray. But there was suddenly a great whale of a fear breaching inside me and falling back with a big splash: I was going to have to sell myself.

I looked out the window, and across a field I saw a cow, standing alone, wondering where the hell she was.

W e were set up in a four-pole tent on the grounds of an estate with the sound of the ocean crashing just outside. I stood on a platform behind a lectern loaned by the local Episcopal Church and I looked out at many of my regulars and some comparably affluent strangers and they were in their boaters and chinos and late spring silks and I looked at all their faces once, twice. Mrs. Fielding was there, near the back. John Paul Gibbons was on the right side in the second row, and he winked at me. This was becoming a discomforting motif. And suddenly I figured I knew whose request it was that I be auctioned off.

I began. To an ancient little lady I did not know—I presumed she was a permanent Hamptons resident—I sold the services of Puff Daddy to hip-hop her answering machine message. I had an order bid in my book for a hundred and fifty but I squeezed six hundred dollars from the old lady, invoking the great, thinking beings-of-the-deep in their hour of need. I'd gotten a cello lesson with Yo-Yo Ma up to sixteen hundred dollars—having ferreted out two sets of parents, each with a child they'd browbeaten into learning the cello—when Trevor appeared at the back of the tent. He lifted his chin at me, as if he was tasting his coffee.

We'd never spoken of this event during the week we'd just spent together. I didn't expect him. I felt something strong suddenly roil up within me, but I wasn't sure what. I focused on the next bid. "It's against the couple down in front. How about seventeen? Seventeen hundred? What if your child meets *their* child in a school music competition?"

They hesitated.

"Whose butt will get whipped?" I cried.

They bid seventeen hundred. But I felt it was over. The other couple was hiding behind the heads in front of them. I scanned the audience a last time. Trevor was circling over to my left. "Fair warning," I called.

There were no more bids and I sold Yo-Yo Ma for one thousand seven hundred dollars as Trevor found a seat. Oddly, I still didn't know how I felt about his being here. I threw myself into the lots on Arthur's list and I was good, I was very good. The whales were no doubt somewhere off the coast leaping for joy. And then I reached lot nineteen.

"The next lot . . ." I began and I felt my throat seizing up. I felt Trevor's dark eyes on me, without even looking in his direction. I was breathless against the wall of the elevator and all I could hear was the bell and the pop of Trevor's breath as he moved and my mind had begun to wander a little bit and he was right about how he smelled whenever he visited his mother's apartment, he smelled of lilacs—no, not of lilacs, of lilac *sachet*—and my head thumped against the wall and I said "Oops" but he did not hear and I thought about her pillows and though I was glad I was not in her bed, I figured I'd accept those dozen pillows on the floor of the elevator so I could lie down in a soft place for this.

"The next lot . . ." I repeated and I pushed on. "Number nineteen. Dinner for two at Fellini's in Soho, with wine and your auctioneer."

There was a smattering of delighted oohs and chuckles.

I almost started the bidding at a measly fifty dollars. But this impulse did not come from my auctioneer self, I instantly realized. There was a shrinking inside me that I did not like and so I started the bid for what I thought to be an exorbitant amount. I'd simply go unclaimed. "Who'll open the bid for four hundred dollars?" I said.

I saw John Paul's head snap a little, but before I could

congratulate myself, in my peripheral vision I could see a paddle leap up without pause. I looked. It was Trevor.

Suddenly there was something I had to know.

I said, "I'm sorry, ladies and gentlemen, let me stop right here for a moment. Before we begin, I need some more information on this lot."

There was a ripple of laughter through the tent and I stepped away from the lectern. Arthur was standing off to my right and I stepped down from the platform and I approached him.

He must have read something in my face. He blanched and whispered, "What is it? You're doing a smashing job."

"Who asked to put me up for bid?"

"Sorry, my dear," he said. "That's a bit of a secret."

"You're starting to sound British again. You know you're in trouble. And you are. Give it up."

He tried to wink and shrug and say nothing.

"Arthur," I said as calmly as I could. "I don't want to grab you by the throat and throw you to the ground in front of all these good clients. Tell me who."

This was convincing. "Trevor Martin," he said.

I felt a flash of anger. Why? I demanded explanations from myself as I stepped back up onto the platform: Surely this was something I wanted. I wanted Trevor to pay big bucks for me and take me to dinner like he should. But what's this "should" stuff about? Why *should* he do that? And why should *I* expect— as part of me did—a sweet and gentle invitation to dinner in an elevator instead of a hot five minutes of sex? I'd been thinking about the sex, myself. I'd been wanting it. I couldn't let myself be a hypocrite.

I cried, "We have four hundred from Mr. Martin. Who'll make it five hundred?" and all the explanations vanished in my head and I was left with an abrupt realization: there was something being put before this crowd that had a value in need of being articulated. I pointed to one of the paddles in the back. It was held by the little man who'd bought the second-rate Renoir, who'd want to talk about heaven knows what over dinner, maybe the time he'd seen his pudgy mama in the nude, after her bath. "Five hundred," I called and that suddenly seemed way too low.

"I am not a Renoir," I said. "But I am . . . not six inches square, either."

It was a start.

"I am in excellent condition," I cried. "For an object my age. Who'll make it a thousand?"

It was a big leap. But I found myself feeling ready for a big leap.

There was only a moment of hesitation and I saw a paddle go up to my right and I looked and it was John Paul Gibbons. All right. "A thousand dollars to John Paul Gibbons. Who'll make it eleven hundred?"

And now I looked to Trevor. He raised his paddle instantly. "Eleven hundred to Mr. Martin. And this is still an unconscionable bargain. I am rare. I am. Who else knows so many of you so well? Who else has filled your homes and emptied your wallets? Who'll make it fifteen hundred?"

I turned back to John Paul and he winked again and lifted his paddle and he glanced over his shoulder toward Trevor.

I said, "I am a perfect size, thanks to my ongoing efforts. Neither too big nor too small. Who'll make it two thousand?"

I also looked at Trevor and he smiled that faintly patronizing smile of his and he lifted his paddle, and I was caught by his smile, the smile that he gave me the first time I saw him, the smile he'd given me as we walked past the doorman last night and into the warm evening air and he said, "I think I've begun to move into the rest of my life."

His life. But what did I want in the rest of *my* life? I'd like to have seen the inside of *his* apartment by this point. I'd like to have been asked to dinner, just the two of us, without a price put on anything. He takes his first step in the elevator, when it's least expected, and he arranges to *buy* his next step. This was his mother's way. I lowered my face. My book lay open before me. I lifted my face. "I am authentic," I said. "You must look into me now, as I've looked into you." And I took my own challenge. And I looked. And I said, "Three thousand to the book."

There was a little gasp. A private tour of Dollywood, Tennessee, with Dolly Parton herself as guide, had gone for twenty-eight hundred, the biggest bid of the auction.

I looked at John Paul. He blew me a little kiss and kept his paddle on his lap. I turned to Trevor. "It's against you, Mr. Martin," I said. "Thirty-five?"

The smile was gone. But he lifted his paddle.

"Three thousand five hundred to Mr. Martin," I cried, and I instantly added, "Four thousand to the book."

Now there was a great hum that lifted in the crowd, resonating, perhaps, with the one from the sea. "It's against you, Mr. Martin," I said. His face slowly eclipsed itself behind the face in front of him, a jowly man in a shirt and tie, a Wall Street lawyer who collected Stieff teddy bears.

"Fair warning," I cried, scanning the faces before me. I let the warning sit with them all for a long moment, and then I said, "Sold to the book for four thousand dollars."

I did not waste any time in fulfilling the bargain. The next Monday night I sat at the newest chic Soho restaurant with the faces of Anita Ekberg and Marcello Mastroianni and Giulietta Masina and Signor Fellini himself all about me on the walls, and two places were set at the table. But I was alone and waiting for no one. And yet, I lingered over the linguini, eating it strand by strand, sipping my wine in tiny, dry sips. The book, of course, had been empty. I'd bid for myself, and I'd won.

And for a time that night at Fellini's, I was uncommonly happy. I enjoyed the manager's confusion about my missing companion. Eventually I told him to take the other place away and I ignored his pitying look without even getting pissed about it. I enjoyed eating slowly. On the night I sold Missy I ate slowly, too. Probably for the first time in my young life and for the last time till this moment. Though I've always eaten even faster when I'm angry, the night of my seventh birthday I was in such a serious rage at all of the people in the other room that I slowed way down. They thought I'd be unhappy with my meal, but boy did I savor the food.

Boy was I savoring this food at Fellini's.

And the thing that had brought me here.

It'd been a grand gesture.

I'd won myself.

So now what?

I got up in the middle of my pasta course and headed toward the ladies' room.

I pushed open the door marked *donne* and stepped in. The rest room was bright and astringent and a man said, "Buona sera."

I looked around sharply and after a brief pause the same voice said, "Good evening." The voice was coming from the ceiling, I realized. And then, after another pause, he repeated, "Buona sera."

He paused again, waiting for me to repeat the phrase.

Fellini's was piping in an Italian language lesson for its peeing diners.

I stepped into a stall and sat and a woman's voice on the tape replied to the man, "Buona sera. Come sta . . . Good evening. How are you? . . . Buona sera. Come sta."

"Bene, grazie," I muttered.

"Bene, grazie," the man said. "Fine, thank you. Bene grazie."

My body clamped up in the presence of this man. I was having trouble doing my business here. And he grew bolder.

"Che professione esercita?" he asked. What's your profession.

I ignored him and tried to relax.

"Sono attrice," the woman answered. "I am an actress."

"Sono attrice," I repeated with her.

"È sposata?" the man asked. "Are you married?"

I wished my Italian wasn't so limited. So while he asked it again in Italian—nagging like my mother—I answered him in English, which he obviously also spoke: "None of your fucking business."

"No, sono nubile," the woman said. "No, I am single. No, sono nubile." The second time she said it in Italian, her voice had gone all gooey.

"Slut," I said.

I hadn't heard the rest room door open and close. A woman just outside the stalls said sharply, "What?"

"Non parlo inglese," I said. I don't speak English.

The woman went into an adjoining stall. I finished my business, did a quick hand-wash, and beat it out of the rest room while the Italian actress with no self-respect agreed to meet this boorish guy for a drink and arranged for him to pick her up at her hotel. As far as I could tell, these two didn't even know each other's name.

When I got back to my table I could see Alain Bouchard getting a drink at the bar.

I sat down before my pasta and stared at it.

I still felt as if I'd done something important.

I twirled some linguine onto my fork.

I glanced up very discreetly and looked out toward the bar.

Alain was being discreet, as well. He leaned against the bar, keeping his profile toward me, angling his head just enough to observe me in a general way in his peripheral vision. I sensed that if I ignored him, he'd quietly slip away.

What the hell was this all about?

What was the appropriate response for a self-possessed woman?

I put my fork down and I raised my face forthrightly to him. I waited for him to realize I was staring at him. He chickened out, turning his profile away from me.

I pushed back, stood up, strode across the dining room and out to the bar and I approached him. I stopped and confronted the back of his head. He did not seem to know I was there. "Monsieur Bouchard," I said.

He bucked and swung around and it was pleasant to see him struggle to turn guilty tumult into routine surprise. He focused tightly on my eyes and smiled. "Hello, Miss Dickerson," he said.

He was taking a breath to say more and I cut him off. "Don't let's get off on the wrong foot," I said. "You're about to say, 'What a surprise,' but that's not quite true, is it?"

"Not quite," he said. "I was surprised when I first walked in, but not just now."

I frowned at this. He picked up on my reservation at once. He said, "Startled, yes. You came upon me very silently."

"So you just happened to wander into Fellini's on the night I'm here?"

"What is the alternative explanation, Miss Dickerson? Am I stalking you?"

"I don't even want to go there," I said.

Alain flickered a bit with incomprehension.

"It's an idiom," I said. "Look, now that you're here and I'm here and I'm clearly interested in who the hell you are, come sit down and bring your drink."

Even I could hear how nasty that sounded. To Alain's credit, he didn't flinch at all at my tone. He nodded and smiled warmly and said, "I'd be delighted."

I led him toward my table and I considered what I'd just said and it was absolutely true in both word and tone. I'd always been pretty blunt, but I wondered if self-possession would effectively remove what little editor there was left in my head. I hoped not.

When we were seated, Alain said, "I trust you don't take my ready acceptance of your invitation as a sign I'd been orchestrating all this."

"Given how bitchy the invitation actually was," I said.

Alain took a deep breath and sat back. In the slight pause that followed, it occurred to me that I should help him out. I figured I'd presented him with two alternatives—blatantly lie to me or openly agree that I'd been a bitch. But as he'd done to us at the lunch with Arthur, I decided to let him dangle.

He was up to the challenge. He said, "My father was a diplomat. Mostly in the Far East. Japan immediately after the war. Indochina a little later. I was conceived, I'm told, in the Hotel Continental in Saigon in the final days of our misbegotten empire. He went to Geneva in 1954 and helped work out the language of the final accord."

Alain leaned forward again and smiled at me, very gently, as if I'd just said something sweet instead of shitty, and I wondered if he was gay. This thought came upon me abruptly, but fortunately the editor in my brain hadn't totally vacated the premises. I needed a long moment, a deep breath, and a sitting back, a concerted act of the will, but I put that whole question aside. Instead, I was about to say, "Would you like to give him a call right now for advice?" But I was even able to intercept that impulse.

Alain sipped his drink and I smiled back at him, carefully matching his warmth, and I said, "My daddy was in cattle and oil in Texas. The oil was his shrewd sideline that made us all very comfortable, but it was the cattle he loved. He didn't run a feedlot. He'd mostly raise them to weanlings, though he did get into the feed stuff for a while, doing yearlings, but either way he'd pamper them and then move them on. You're looking at a lady who can smell cow shit in the air and get misty-eyed for her childhood."

I could feel Alain being careful with all this. He waited to make sure I'd finished and then he said, still soft-edged, "For me, it is traffic fumes."

I didn't understand for a moment.

"To become misty-eyed," he said. "The traffic of Paris. As a boy, I would walk to my school along the Boulevard St. Germaine and I loved the automobiles, of course, the Citroens in particular. The smell of the automobile exhaust is my cow shit."

"You're lucky," I said. "I don't smell much cow shit around New York. Only metaphorically. You have plenty of cars."

"Ah, but it hasn't been quite the same in America since the catalytic converter, I'm afraid."

"I'm sorry."

We fell silent again and I looked at my food.

"It grows cold," he said.

I glanced up at him and he nodded toward my pasta.

I noticed the manager hovering at the edge of my vision and I turned to him and Alain did too. The manager asked, "Shall I set a place for signore?"

Alain looked at me briefly but made up his own mind. "No. Thank you. I won't be staying."

I thought to contradict this, but before I could, the manager vanished and Alain leaned a little closer and said, "I don't mean to intrude. Really. Though I do admit I was curious to see who had recognized your excellent value at the auction."

I didn't know how to read this admission, or the slightly heavy-handed compliment. And I hadn't seen him in the Hamptons. "Were you there?"

"No. But I heard from Arthur."

With his use of the familiar "Arthur" I decided that if his curiosity was not idle, it was simply professional. He was gay.

"So how far out of your way did you go to see?" I asked.

"Not far. I've taken an apartment a few blocks along."

"And you were just walking by. Like in your schoolboy days."

"Yes. Just so."

I nodded at Alain and wished he'd go away. My focus on him drifted. I looked out toward the front of the restaurant and a vaguely familiar figure was approaching the bar. Vague because the face was obscured by a trilby hat pulled down low and by his body being angled away, awkwardly. Alain said something I missed. I looked at him again, though I was feeling an oddly morbid intuition about the figure at the bar.

"What was that?" I said to Alain.

"Did he stand you up?"

The man at the bar was peeking this way from under the brim of his hat.

"No," I said. "I wasn't stood up."

"I see."

"Do you?"

I was good at identifying people from a distance. It was part of my job. This guy was making a serious effort not to be recognized.

"Yes, I see," Alain said. "You weren't stood up."

"And what do you think that means?" I said.

"Did you . . . Could that . . ."

Alain was off balance, groping around for words, a state I'd not seen him in. But I couldn't concentrate on enjoying that. I was distracted by the man in the trilby hat.

Alain suddenly laughed loud. The man at the bar looked toward the sound and he showed a little too much of his face. It was Trevor.

"You bid for yourself," Alain said.

I focused intently on Alain now. I'd not spoken with Trevor since the auction. He didn't yet know he'd been dumped. For a moment I was glad that Alain was here. If Trevor was so curious, let him think he'd been outbid by this handsome, distinguished, expensively clothed and coiffed man with an elegant way of shaping his words before him with his hands as he spoke, and with something else, a je ne sais quoi. Why was I suddenly angry at Arthur? I was. But I wasn't, surely. For Arthur, I realized, it was a thing more like jealousy. In fact my anger was for Trevor. More so now, with him spying on me. I was angry at Alain too, it occurred to me. Neither of them should be here.

"You know," I said, "I've got to leave now."

"Surely not," Alain said, his hands spreading before him. And then they dropped to the table as if they'd been shot. "I have spoiled your moment," he said.

I grabbed my purse and rose. "Not at all. You're absolved of all guilt." I made a little cross in the air before him, a gesture that surprised the hell out of both of us. I hadn't even noticed how his hands moved when he talked, not till a few moments ago. "I have to go."

And I went. Along the tables and into the bar and Trevor was using the same hunch-up tactic that Alain had used earlier and I almost passed him by without a word. Perhaps it would have been best if I did. But I didn't. I veered over to him and leaned close to the back of his head. "Buona sera," I said. "None of your fucking business. Grazie. Arrivederci."

He did not even turn around.

I often don't know where I am in the streets of New York. I can find my way up or down or across or whatever, but for all the attention to the detail of things in my work, I'm vague about the streets of the city. I like that. I went out of Fellini's and I walked up the island for a time and then across and then back down a ways. Not that I wasn't taking it all in. It was a spring night. I spent a few minutes checking my back, not for muggers—Giuliani had made all this more or less safe again—but for Alain or Trevor or whoever else, Arthur or John Paul Gibbons or the young Mover and Lifter with bad skin who always gave me a wink when he passed me at the office—the two boys at Fellini's had made me paranoid for a few minutes—but the paranoia didn't last, and after those few minutes of checking my back and seeing—

thank god—no one I knew, I relaxed. I was happy to find that the pleasure I'd felt when I first sat down alone at the dinner table tonight had returned. It was a late spring night and I was alone in the streets of New York City. Drifting. A long row of quiet terra-cotta and brownstone, shadows of sweetgum and ginkgo and honey locust in the spill of streetlight on the stoops. Lit panes of tableaux: a wall of books, a dragonfly Tiffany lamp, a jumble of sedately partying bodies with laughter and a Sidney Bechet soprano sax riff coming out to me. Another street, a clinking of glasses, hands held across a sidewalk table, Marilyn Monroe edged in red neon, a bookstore window full of Susie Bright and Annie Sprinkle and a hello from the doorway. A corner, a Korean deli, cut flowers spilling out the front, and I went in and filled a plastic box with dollops from the round-the-clock buffet—I was still hungry—a pound and a half of sesame noodles and spicy tofu and sweet-and-sour chicken nuggets and three-bean salad and gyoza and seaweed and stuffed grape leaves and samosa and coleslaw. And then I took a cab home, my snack in my lap. I was happy again.

Even standing in the center of my apartment, which was too quiet and fraught with associations. There were four messages on my answering machine. I ignored them for a while. I sat on the stool at my pass-through and ate my dollops, starting off keeping them separate, carefully moving from one to the other, managing the sequence of tastes, but eventually just mixing them all together, speeding up. Eating too fast. Old habits die hard.

I started trying to guess the four. Trevor. It took all this to make him call. Alain. I left him abruptly and it was possible he wasn't a jerk and he was concerned. But did he know my home phone number? Of course. He was about to buy the whole company, me included. Yow. That thought stopped me. I was still up for sale.

My plastic box was empty and I didn't remember taking the last bite.

I got up, approached the machine, the red 4 burning brightly in the dark. Trevor. Alain. Probably Arthur—I hadn't seen him today, my first opportunity since the charity auction. He had to be curious. In fact, I was surprised he hadn't shown up casing Fellini's, as well. Arthur would be on the machine. And my mother was due.

I got three out of four. Trevor's voice was odd. He seemed very stiff, not used to talking to the machine. I thought of his mother. Surely she'd always resisted these machines. And Trevor one day would regret selling all her stuff. He'd start collecting his own Victoriana, end up sleeping with lilac sachets. "Amy," he said. "I'm sorry. It wasn't what you thought. You've touched every object around me, finding its value. Come touch me again. You found a flaw, but my value isn't ruined. Please at least call me. Let me explain."

He took another breath after that, as if to say more, but what I touched was the erase button and the nasally fussbudget of a man who lived in the machine said, "Press erase again." I did and he said, "Message erased," and I felt good.

Then there was Alain. "I hope I did not cause you some distress. I stopped in to Fellini's on the way to my apartment because I'd heard of the place from the auction, yes, but I did not know you would be there. Forgive me for intruding."

That was the end of the message and I found myself waiting for some little something more. Would you give me a call?
Hope to see you again. At least, Perhaps we'll run into each other
at Nichols and Gray. Something. But this was fine. He was probably having a drink or whatever with Arthur.

Next was Mother. "Honey, I was just sitting here worrying about you. I hope you're out having a good time all these
nights. It's lonely here. Houston just keeps on growing. I talked
with Missy today. She seems so happy in her life. Do you still
give her a call? We're both so proud of how busy and important you are, Sweetie. Please call me when you have a chance.
I love you to smithereens. Bye now."

This was pretty typical of her phone talk to me. She was
better in person. Just as disapproving, ultimately, but a little
less obvious about it. I pushed the erase button. Sometimes you
can just tell by hearing a couple of people speak that they're
right for each other: I suddenly thought about getting Mama
together with the nasally fussbudget asking me to push the
button again.

The idea passed and I did what he said and I expected to
hear from Arthur next, but this time I was wrong. It was Missy.
"Hi Amy. I just want to apologize for my attitude at our last
lunch. Maybe this guy is the one you've been waiting for. Didn't
I have an intuition something like that about Jeffrey? Try to find
him, why don't you. Go for it. And listen, in the meantime, why
don't you come out this weekend? The girls haven't seen you
in a while. Jeffrey either. We'd all love to have you. Please come."

"Missy, you jerk," I said softly to the machine.

I threw myself onto the couch and I wasn't quite sure who I was mad at. Missy was clueless. She bitched at me when I was looking for support and supported me only after I'd moved on. But how could she have expected that in the less than two weeks since our lunch, Dark Eyes would have gone from anonymity to soulful confidences to a fuck in an elevator to the revelation of a fatal flaw to the great Dumpster of Doomed Relationships? And whose fault was that? Mine, sure. I was clueless too. Had Trevor been that hard to read? And he was clueless. Right then. Sitting in his mama's apartment waiting for me to return his call.

I pressed my eyes shut. This was the wrong way to think of all this, I knew. I was happy just a little while ago. Walking alone in the night. A clinking of glasses. Hands held across a table on the street. I'd turned to look as I passed. A car honked somewhere. His hand was on top of hers, there alongside the basket of bread sticks. Trevor was done with. What was the point of an active ill-feeling? We'd had a good moment. His hand falling gently on top of mine with my head still sprocketing faintly from his mother's toy. If I owned myself now, I owned every good moment, no matter what happened before or after. I looked at Trevor's hand on mine and it was a large hand, with a faint scar, like a question mark, between the first and second knuckle. The center of his palm was soft. Max's palm was rougher. Not rougher, exactly. I shifted on the couch now, turned a little on my side, flexed my legs beneath me. Max's palm wasn't rough. It was tight. Nice tight, like his back muscles when his arms were around me. But he could be gentle with these palms. I let myself go to nipple-memory. Max would lay his tight palms on my breasts and my nipples would lift to him, he'd let my nipples do the pressing. I could not think of the moment when Trevor touched my breasts. There was no such moment. I regretted that. I would like to have a memory on my nipples of his soft palm. But there was his palm touching the back of my hand while eight metal jockeys looked on. Fred's palm was soft, too, like the silk of his nightshirt. He'd run his palm lightly across the tip of my nipple, and it was the brush of silk, faintly cool, a spun thing, not flesh at all. And Fred's fingers were long. He played the piano some and I'd imagined when we were together—after he'd spoken once, dismissively, of the lessons he'd taken as a boy—that his teacher, a woman, had held his boy's hands in hers and envied how long these fingers were already. Fred's fingernails were elongated, too, the shape of oval-cut diamonds.

What mood was this that had come upon me? There were, inside me, the precisely delineated memories of the hands of other men, as well, I realized. More vivid than faces. What was the thing Alain had said? The rich variety of life? I was, it seemed, a collector.

When I finally encountered Arthur, Wednesday morning, I'd just stepped into the elevator and he tried to make a U-turn when he saw me. No one else was coming or going at that moment. I held the door and said his name, once, sharply.

He stopped and turned back to me sheepishly. "Hello,

dear," he said. "I was just going to . . . ah . . . check something with the security fellow over there."

I knew the real problem. "Come on, Arthur, you don't have to be afraid of me."

He made a vague gesture toward the heavyset man in a uniform reading the *Daily News* at the front-lobby desk. "Well, perhaps it can wait."

"Arthur."

"All right."

He stepped in.

I wasn't critical of his little lie. After all, the last time we'd been together I'd threatened to grab him by the throat and throw him to the ground. Arthur clearly took my threat seriously. I liked him for that.

I pushed our floor button and the doors closed and I said, "I'm sorry I threatened you, Arthur."

"What's that? No, no. All is forgiven. Never taken seriously, really. You're a rascal, Amy. You got Trevor Martin's name out of me. But he didn't win, did he? Not at all. Someone in the book? Yes?"

"Arthur you've gone straight to stage three this time, talking like a Dickens character. You're under a lot of stress."

"Yes I am, as a matter of fact. Your Mr. Bouchard is a hard bargainer."

"*My* Mr. Bouchard?"

"He adores you. That's clear."

The elevator stopped and the door opened on our suite of offices. Arthur stepped briskly out. I followed, but he was already striding away. "Must run," he said.

"To phone the desk cop?"

Arthur wobbled his head in response as he receded as if to say, Oh you know that was a lie.

I was left with Arthur's impression that Alain adored me. I suppose there was a flicker in me that suggested he *adored-me* adored me. But that was gone instantly—the comment had been linked to hard bargaining, and I understood it to mean I was a greatly desirable asset. Alain was going to have to deal with that eventually. I needed an offer, money, a stake in the new company. Something.

In the nick of time I caught myself mumbling audibly. I'd just come into view of Lydia and I didn't want her panicking over my sanity. She was hunched over the computer. I slowed as I neared, hoping she wasn't porning on the Internet or playing solitaire. I liked Lydia. I liked her pessimism, somehow. I wanted her to do well in her job, in her life, in contradiction of all her worst expectations. I wondered if that kind of success would make her miserable. I stopped at her desk. She surely knew I was nearby but she had not altered her demeanor one bit for me. This emboldened me to look at her computer screen and she was piecing together a boilerplate solicitation letter for me. "Good," I said.

"What's good?" she said, not looking up at me.

"Ah . . . Well, good, yes." I sounded like Arthur in my awkwardness. But I didn't want to tell her, Good you're not goofing off so I won't have to start working myself up to fire you. "Good *work*," I finally said. "You're getting that solicitation letter done."

"Lousy work," she said. "This stuff stinks."

This time she didn't ask if she was free to speak her mind. I was touched at her trust in me.

"You're right," I said. "If you can improve on any of it, give it a try."

"Really?"

"Yes."

"I might."

She hunched forward again and I glanced at her desktop, and there was a five-by-seven color photo half tucked under her folded *New York Times*. It was a child. Lydia and I had not gotten this far yet. It might be hers. It might not. I was about to slip away into my office. Lydia sensed it.

"Call slips in the middle of your desk pad," she said.

"Thanks, yes," I said, but something about the pudgy fingers splayed there near the *Times* made me say, "Lydia, is that your baby?"

"Are you looking at the picture?" she asked without turning. She was moving text around on her screen.

"On your desk," I said. "Yes."

"Yes."

"May I?"

"Sure."

I picked the photo up.

I had a nightmare once. I was behind the podium, ready to start an auction. I didn't know of what. Sometimes I have nightmares based on that alone. I'm about to start an auction and I realize I've failed even to find out what's being offered. I know nothing about the stuff and I'm like an actress who forgot to learn her lines, a dream I also have now and then. But in this particular nightmare it didn't bother me, not knowing the offerings. Instead, the problem was that I looked out at the bidders and they were all babies. Every chair in the room—and the room was deep, going back into distant shadows—every chair had a baby sitting in it and every baby was focused intently on me and I couldn't read their faces at all. And this terrified me. They all looked alike. Poochy cheeks, wide eyes, wispy-haired pink domes. You can read an adult's personal subtext, hidden agendas, secret cravings, but a baby's face is as fundamental and uninflected as poop and pee.

In short, my nightmare was made up of baby's faces that looked exactly like the face in this picture. Not that I didn't have a warm, kootchy-under-the-chin feeling, as well. The baby was adorable. It was dressed in black and had tiny bloodred earrings in its pierced ears. "She's wonderful," I said.

"Her name is Winter." Lydia had turned away from the computer and was looking up at me now.

"Is she a happy baby?" I was wondering if Lydia's gloom was strictly Goth-cultural or if it was somehow genetic.

"So far."

"That's good, yes?"

Lydia knew what I as driving at. "It's good to be happy. *I'm* happy, Ms. Dickerson," she said, her mouth turned down, her eyes lifted to me like Mary suffering at the foot of the cross.

"Are you with Winter's father?" I asked, figuring the speaking-your-mind thing could go either direction.

"Sort of."

"Well, she's beautiful."

"Do you have any children, Ms. Dickerson?"

"No."

"Oh." Lydia sounded disappointed, like she'd hoped I'd be a source of firsthand advice.

"My sister has two girls I'm very close to. I know what it's all about."

"I get so angry at some things," Lydia said. "Like mosquitoes, for instance. I just want to stay in the city because if you go out to where there's trees and water and stuff, these monsters are all around in the air trying to suck her blood. It's like a vampire thing. But I get scared even worse than at the movies, 'cause it's your *baby* they're after. Not even the scariest movies send the vampire after a baby."

I looked at Winter. She was smiling, showing two tiny teeth. I could understand Lydia's concern, creatures after this baby's blood.

"And you can't even spray, like, Black Flag or anything," Lydia said. "The poison'd go through her pores or into her lungs and there you are."

"So you just keep away from the trees and so forth?"

"Sure. That's just fine, except in the city you've got the cockroaches and the rats and some jerk dancing around your apartment on Ecstasy knocking over furniture and thinking your baby wants to be thrown up in the air and caught. Which Winter laughs about, and that's a whole other thing, me worrying she's going to grow up to be a slut."

A feeling was starting to come on me like in those nightmares. I stood there utterly unprepared for what was expected of me. But I did manage to say, "All babies like to be thrown into the air, I think. It doesn't mean anything."

Lydia shrugged. "We'll see."

Now I was definitely out of advice. I placed Winter's picture on the desk, gently, and I said, "She's a wonderful baby."

Lydia squared the picture around before her. "She's got her
daddy's eyes."

It wasn't clear to me whether that was supposed to be a
good thing or a bad thing, and I didn't inquire. Lydia took us
both off the hook. "Well, back to work," she said and she turned
to her computer screen. I escaped into my office.

I sat at my desk and all around me were heavy oak shelves
filled with books about the world of collectible objects. I loved
the preparation for the auctions, the deep plunge into the world
of *things,* and I swiveled in my chair to look at the familiar row
of terra-cotta lion heads across the street, and all I wanted to
do now was think about Utamaro woodblock prints, dragonfly
Tiffany lamps, Quimper pitchers, Allen & Ginter tobacco tins,
a fully restored Hispano Suiza drophead coupe, a 1952 Topps
Mickey Mantle, the Boni and Liveright true first edition of
Hemingway's *In Our Time.* Whatever. Things. I just wanted to
do my work. But there was messy stuff in the way. With all the
bits and pieces of wisdom about auctioneering rattling around
in my head, I'd somehow lost the one about never fucking your
clients. I wasn't going to be able to simply ignore Trevor's calls.
I had to get this over with. I pulled up his file on my computer
and found his business phone number. Better to talk with him
there. For a moment I thought of the alternative, and I pictured
him speaking to me in the midst of all his mother's things. But
he didn't live at her place. There had to be a Trevor apartment
somewhere. The fact that such a place existed and I'd never been

there—it had never even been referred to, between us—made me even more angry at the way he'd handled things.

I dialed and his secretary seemed to know my name, instantly putting me through, and that made me angrier still. He said, "Amy. I'm desperately happy you've called."

"Desperately?"

"I know something's suddenly changed between us, in a bad way. I'm afraid it's my fault somehow."

I turned to the window again. It was a lousy view. I deserved better. These lions roared on forever, quietly, dispassionately. They could well have been yawning. This struck me quite vividly now. They were fucking yawning.

"Amy?"

I'd been silent for these moments while I thought about my Greek chorus of lions, yawning a commentary on my life. But what I was really doing was avoiding going on in this conversation. My impulse was to explain to Trevor what had happened. How thoroughly he'd blown it. How I'd come to make an important choice about myself. It was his fault *somehow*? Either he was clueless or pretending to be so and I had no interest in telling him anything important. Not to mention I was only beginning to figure out what that choice meant for me.

"You walked out on him, too," Trevor said.

I didn't understand what he was talking about. Then it struck me. My abrupt departure at Fellini's. He thought Alain had been the winner of the auction.

"Look," I said. "The whole elevator thing was a big mistake. Like the cable snapping or something. You're a client. We've got a bias against clients fucking the staff here. No hard feelings, Mr. Martin, but I'd really like to get us back on a professional footing."

Now it was his turn to be silent. I thought I could hear him breathing. It was measured, cool. Finally he said, "You gave me plenty of signs . . . "

"Did it sound as if I was laying blame? I wasn't. It's nobody's fault."

"That's not my point, Amy." He purred this out and I had the faintest little tremolo of regret at putting the man aside.

It ceased at once. Still, with the prospect of a drawn-out discussion before me, which I had no stomach for at all, I offered a gambit. "I'd rather us not even talk about this anymore, at least until the auction of your mother's things is over."

"That's reasonable," he said. "You're right, of course, about needing to remain professional through this event. Till it's over, then."

"Till it's over."

He hung up without another word. I'd put him off, but not for long. Fair warning.

I sat sweating on the train to Missy's that Saturday—it was a diesel that ran the Jamaica–Oyster Bay route and the air-conditioning was on the fritz and the open door of the car just brought in more heat—and I thought about how I'd not seen or talked to Alain all week. I wondered why I hadn't sought him out one way or the other, since he was pretty clearly waiting for that, still feeling that he'd intruded on Monday night. The ragged run of the Long Island Rail Road right-of-way clicked past outside and I was tired of thinking about all this. Maybe Missy's way was the best. I resolved to keep my mind open this weekend.

They all met me at the Sea Cliff station. Missy and Maggie and Molly and Jeff and their BMW SUV and their bichon frise Matilda. My visits were just infrequent enough that each time I was greeted, I was awhirl in what felt like first impressions. All but the pup were on the platform, though Molly, who was six, seemed to have learned some moves from her pet, breaking from the rest when I came down the steps from the train car and bouncing up and down pawing at me to pick her up. Which I did, with pleasure. "Aunt Amy Aunt Amy," she cried throwing her arms around me, "save me from my horrible sister."

"Molly," Missy said sharply.

Even as I pressed Molly to me, I winked at Maggie, not wanting to take sides in a battle that was much more covert the last time I was here. Maggie, ten now and newly gangly, was standing a little apart, near her dad, and she winked back at me. The restraint of her gesture was also new.

"Molly," Missy snapped again, stepping forward and grabbing at her. "Don't jump on your aunt. You're too big for that."

Molly was peeled off me and deposited on the platform and Missy and I leaned forward at the waist and bussed each other on the cheek. When we straightened up away from each other, Jeff began his approach, opening his arms for a hug that was always just a little too tight and lingering, to my mind, though he'd never flirted with me, really. He was closing in on me now. He was a reasonably handsome man in a gaunt, patrician sort of way, but his eyes were slightly too small for his face—

very nearly *beady*—and they were fixed determinedly on mine.
Then his face slid past and his arms came around me. I braced
myself, returned the hug left-handed only.

"Good to see you, Amy," he said.

I grunted an assent and I felt the fingers on my right hand,
which hung at my side with my overnight bag, being pried open.
Jeff had my face trapped on the wrong shoulder to look, but he
finally let me go and Maggie had my bag. I turned to her and
offered a hug, which she took demurely. She was way taller than
the last time. At the end of our I'm-a-young-lady-now embrace,
she whispered, "Don't believe anything she says," not waiting
for an answer but pulling away and slinging my bag over her
shoulder and moving on ahead of us. I presumed she meant
Molly.

And so we were off to the BMW, which was new, and
Matilda's greeting, which consisted mainly of leaping into my
lap in the backseat and trying to lick up my nostrils. "Oh gross,
Matilda," Maggie said, leaning across Molly, who was between
us, and tugging at the bichon, who I'm sure wanted to be a wildly
shaggy little dog but who Missy kept carefully groomed like the
show dogs, sharply modeled like a topiary. Going up the nose
was probably compensatory behavior for her. She did not yield
to Maggie.

"Here, Matilda," Molly said, brushing her sister out of the
way and offering her own nose, which Matilda took one look
at and joyfully began to ream.

"Gross gross gross," Maggie chanted, turning away from
the spectacle.

"Stop that, Molly," Missy cried from the front seat.

"It's love," Molly said as loud as she could with Matilda in her face.

"It's gross," said Maggie.

"It's Matilda loving me." Molly gasped for breath.

"Do you like the new SUV?" Jeff asked, looking briefly over his shoulder at me.

"She can love you another way," Missy said.

"It's great," I replied to Jeff.

"Oh, Matilda, I love you so much," Molly said extricating her nose and hugging the bichon close.

"I waited for the Beemer," Jeff said. "I thought they'd never introduce it."

Matilda started barking.

"All girls shut up!" Missy cried.

"It still has that new-car smell," Jeff said. I figured the floor of the stock exchange taught him how to keep his focus in the midst of chaos.

Matilda barked louder and Molly started barking with her and so it went, up the hill and along Sea Cliff Avenue to my sister's house.

Which was a late Queen Anne that rambled in its multiple-personality disorder all over its lot, with Norman towers and Romanesque arches and fish-scale cedar shingles and verandas all around. Inside, I tried not to look too closely at Missy and Jeff's things. It was like seeing the two of them stepping from a shower naked, out of shape, overweight, and their hair plastered to their faces. In their decorating tastes they were, to put it gently, eclectic. In the parlor, where I was parked for a long while, I could not avoid registering the Federal eagles in the wallpaper and a large and intricately patterned braid rug—the work of an idiot savant of a grandmother on speed—and Sheraton side tables flanking a vast scimitar of a leather couch with recliners built in at each end. The recliners triangulated a black hulk of a TV with a screen nearly as big as my apartment door. And it was ready for digital, as Jeff pointed out when we toured the new stuff in the room.

I sat in the center of the couch while Molly brought me her every doll, one by one, and I addressed each by its name. And she brought me her school artwork, piece by piece, sunny skies and solitary little girls with white dogs. After showing each thing to me she scrambled around the curve of the couch to her father, who sat at one of the recliners with his feet up. Each time I visited he'd have occasion to grab Molly onto his lap and run minor variations on the same words: That's swell/ great/ terrific, Pumpkin/ Sweetheart/ Mollymonster. This visit, it was swell and Pumpkin. Meanwhile, Maggie was perched on a blue velvet wing-back chair across the room, watching the spectacle, occasionally observing, dryly, "That's *my* doll, actually." Molly ignored her. I caught Maggie's eye a couple of times to give her another wink, but mostly it was Molly at the center of the universe. Missy would stick her head in now and then to remind us how sad she was to be missing the fun but she was working real hard in the kitchen to make our great dinner. I offered several times to come and help—Maggie, to her credit, even offered once, as well—but Missy emphatically rejected these offers. Each time Molly scampered off to get another object for our examination, I'd ask Maggie questions—about school; about her friends; about soccer, which I knew she'd been doing—but she'd answer only very briefly, as if these were secrets that she and I shared and I should know better than to bring them up in front of others. And over all this Jeff kept his own conversational track going with me—about stocks; about the international balance of trade; about that monster digital-ready TV there before us; about football, which he forgot whether or not I followed but how 'bout them Dawgs, meaning, I vaguely remembered, the bulldogs of the University of Georgia, where he'd been a business major even as an undergraduate. And speaking of dogs, in the midst of all this, Matilda did what I was told was common to her breed, something called the "bichon buzz," a wild, top-speed race around and around the room and out into the hallway and beyond and back again, growling in faux viciousness all the while, with a dog-toy clamped in her mouth, often dashing out with one toy and reentering with another from some unseen cache of them—a latex hamburger or octopus or carrot or foot—the toy squeaking in protest—and Molly joined in, chasing her pup until Matilda finally wore out abruptly and dropped the toy and threw herself onto her back in the middle of the parlor floor. As Molly crouched over her, rubbing Matilda's tummy, I decided that the pup in fact was deeply in touch with a cosmic truth about the way life is lived on the planet Earth and she had simply acted it out for us. Growling, running, grabbing toys. You got that right, girl.

As Molly cooed over Matilda, and Jeff headed off on some point about the University of Georgia endowment office, I looked over to Maggie and we knew it was time, she and I. We both rose and headed for the door. Simultaneously, I said to Jeff, "I'm going to visit with Maggie now" and Maggie said to Molly, "You've had her long enough."

Maggie's room was a sweet mixture of child and young woman, a bed full of stuffed animals, a perpetually burning Little Mermaid nightlight, posters of Britney Spears and the Backstreet Boys, her computer whirring away showing her My-Yahoo home page. We were in a corner of the third floor and she had a tower alcove, where she led me by the hand after closing and locking her door.

We sat on the built-in bench with more stuffed animals and the tops of maples and walnuts quaking outside the window and she drew her legs up and put her chin on her knees and she didn't start talking right away. I was touched by that, and I kept the silence with her. We watched out the window together for a few moments. A blue jay darted past and Maggie turned her head to follow its flight. She said, "Did you know that blue jays can talk as good as mynah birds, if you catch them and train them? Though you can't, since it's illegal to keep a songbird."

"I didn't know that," I said. "About blue jays."

"I sometimes think I'm living with a family of blue jays," Maggie said, gravely. "Though, like, somebody's taught them how to say some things, which they do over and over."

"And you got yourself into the wrong nest?"

"Yes."

We fell silent together for a few more moments and then I said, "Since you're not a blue jay, if I tell you something, you're not going to repeat it."

"I'm a swan," she said. "Swans don't even have a voice."

I wanted to say something encouraging about this. Impulsively I almost said, But they're very beautiful, but I stopped myself. That was part of the bullshit I'd recently wiped off my own shoes. Before I could think of something else, Maggie took over the point.

"They can be fierce, though," she said. "They hiss."

"You can hiss."

"I hiss a lot."

"I like that," I said. "A hissing beauty."

Maggie giggled at this. I giggled with her. Then she said, "So tell me the secret."

"You're four years older than Molly," I said. "Well, I'm four years older than your mama. When we were growing up, she and I fought all the time."

"Really?"

"Really. She was always elbowing her way into the center of things."

"Mama?"

"Yes."

"And I'm like you?"

She asked this with such a sudden brightness in her eyes and lilt in her voice that I leaned forward and kissed her on the cheek. Then I drew back and I said, "Yes. Like me. I loved my daddy very much—that was your Grandpa Dickerson—but he was always putting your mama on his lap and making little googoo sounds at her and it drove me crazy."

"Oh, Aunt Amy," Maggie said and it was her turn to do a kiss on the cheek. This time we turned it into a hug and before she let go, Maggie said, "Do you still can't stand her?"

I hadn't expected this question, would never have started this whole thing if I thought I'd have to answer it. But instantly I said, "No, sweetie, no. Everything's fine now."

What else was I going to tell a ten-year-old?

So, the dinner. Jeff said grace, which surprised me because Missy hadn't talked about going back to church. I thought she'd left that behind in Houston, as I did. I was sure of it. It was one of those rare things that we saw eye-to-eye on. When we'd argue about men or Mama or mascara we could always turn to religion to get us away from controversy. Oh I believe in God all right, she'd say. Oh me too, I'd say. It's just that the churches believe more in themselves, she'd say. That's so true, I'd say, they worship the worshiping. They worship an image of their own self-righteousness, she'd say. They'd better pray they're wrong about God, I'd say, He's on record as going pretty hard on that. Right, she'd say. "Oh dear God," Jeff said, "thank you for this food and this good fellowship within our family."

He prayed with his eyes open and looking sort of partway up the wall toward the ceiling. Missy had her head bowed. So did the girls, sort of, though Maggie shot me a quick glance to check on my attitude, which was a little bit bent over at the waist, my face angled slightly down but with a good view still of everyone else. Molly had her fingers intertwined tightly before her, and she was looking sideways away from the table, probably trying to find Matilda, who was in fact sitting at my feet. Matilda was also checking out my attitude—about doling out table scraps, not religion, though perhaps the two were tantamount for her.

I was ready to give her plenty, for Missy had prepared chicken pot pie and mashed potatoes and a green bean casserole with mushroom soup and canned onion rings on top. This was definitely a page out of our mama's cookbook. "Dear Father, help those who are hungry," Jeff said and I thought I heard Matilda moan faintly. "Help those who have no family," he said. Next I expected, Help those whose portfolios are overcommitted in new technology, but instead he wrapped it up quickly. "In Jesus' name. Amen."

We all lifted our eyes and checked each other out with wan smiles, and the eating commenced. Molly jabbered, Matilda begged, Maggie ate in silence, and I watched Missy and Jeff as closely as I could without being obvious about it. Clearly, new things had come upon them since I saw them last, and I wanted to try to assess the effects.

Jeff sat at the head of the table and Missy was at his right side, next to me. At some point he'd put his hand on hers on the tabletop and said, "Good job, Honey. It's delicious." He said it rather low and he didn't insist on the girls chiming in. It seemed like a sincere, private moment. At another point Missy dabbed at Jeff's cheek with her napkin, blotting off a bit of mushroom soup—whether from the green bean casserole or from the chicken pot pie, I don't know; cream of mushroom soup was to Missy as olive oil was to Italians—and the gesture seemed a tender one, which he received with a smile.

And after dinner Jeff declared, "Okay girls"—by which he meant Molly and Maggie—"let's give the other sisters a chance for some quality time. Let's do the dishes."

Missy looked faintly surprised but she patted Jeff on the spot where the mushroom soup had been and she said, "Thanks, Sweetie."

A nd so Missy and I ended up on a bench at the top of the cliff at the western edge of Sea Cliff's one square mile. We looked across the harbor and out into Long Island Sound. The day was fading. The first lights were barely visible across the water, far off in New Rochelle and Larchmont. We'd sat here once or twice before. The tone of our conversation seemed to change, slightly, perhaps from the presence of the water, perhaps from not having to look at each other. I even wanted, at times, to put my arm around my sister. I did love her. I loved Mama. And Daddy, of course. I guess loving Daddy was pretty much what all the crap between Missy and me was about. The crap with Mama, too, though the *loving* part got pretty complicated there. This was the stuff in my head with the sound of the trees rustling around Missy and me, and the sailboat bells tinkling below us in the harbor, and behind us, the occasional slow turn of a car at the end of Sea Cliff Avenue and its descent down to the water.

"You have two great girls," I said.

"That's what it's all for."

I looked at her. She kept her eyes out to the distant shore. "All what?" I asked.

"All everything," she said. "You do it all for the kids."

I waited and she said no more, essentially refusing to answer my question about what the *all* was that you did for your kids. Missy's Mighty Armor of Family seemed as if it had a wee chink, and her letting me see it, especially without instantly covering it up when I pressed her, surprised the hell out of me. But maybe she was just exasperated over the girls fighting.

I looked out to where she looked: a flat, slate-gray stretch of water, a rim of faraway land. Then she said, "Did you figure out who the guy was?"

So much for having the edge on Missy. She'd let her guard down for a moment but now she was counterpunching. I didn't want to get into the matter of Trevor, so I stalled. "The guy?"

"The one you fell for at the auction."

"I just let that go," I said, which was true. It was all she needed to know. "It was no big thing."

"No?"

"No."

"Okay. It just sounded like something at lunch." She put a faint drag of sarcasm in the "something."

"It wasn't."

I felt Missy shrug. I was ready to ignore that, but she had to take it another step, my sister. "Is it ever?" she said.

"Ever what." It wasn't a question. I was saying, If you're going to do your self-righteous critical thing, then at least say it all.

"Something."

"Meaning?"

"Forget it."

I imagined her in her crazy-quilt home. The couch was new. Leather furniture was Jeff's taste. The girls were asleep. Jeff sat with his feet up on one recliner, and along the vast curve of that couch, at the distant other end, Missy sat with her feet up on the other recliner. The television was on. The room was filled with a sitcom laugh track in surround-sound. Jeff had the zapper. This was something?

I said, "I do not know which to prefer, the bitchiness of inflections or the bitchiness of innuendoes."

"What does that mean?"

"Forget it," I said.

"Another thing," Missy said. "Mama didn't hate Daddy."

It took me a moment to realize that this was another issue at our last lunch. Usually our get-togethers didn't take quite this toll on her, at least not that I'd ever been aware of. I said, "Of course she hated him."

"What makes you think so?"

"All you'd have to do was look at how they sat in a room together." Only after I'd said this did I realize I was testing my little vision of Missy's marriage.

Missy made a tiny sucking sound and she shifted away from me ever so slightly and I knew I was right. I didn't feel guilty about my bitchy innuendo, but I hadn't meant to draw this much blood. It was one sort of deed to attack a sister for all the things she doesn't have and another sort of deed to attack a sister for the only thing she does. Still, I didn't know how to close the wound. We were silent for a long, squirmy moment, and then Missy said, very softly, "You trust too much to that auctioneer baloney of yours, trying to read people by little signs that don't mean shit."

I could not remember the last time Missy had said "shit." It might have been when I primed her to say it at her fourth birthday party. It definitely was time for me to start back-pedaling now.

"She loved him," Missy said.

"Sure," I said.

"You don't mean it," Missy said.

"I mean it," I said.

"So you were wrong?"

She was pushing this too hard. She knew not to do that. "There was a time when she loved him," I said.

"And then she started hating him, you're saying."

"What difference does it make now? He's dead."

"Right. So stop saying Mama hated him."

"Look, nobody hates anyone in our family," I said, though I carefully chose my verb tenses. "We all love each other."

"Sure," Missy said. It was a hard little nut of a word.

The water was growing dark out there before us. A dog barked somewhere over the edge of the cliff.

"I love you like a sister," Missy said.

It had come to that. "Me too," I said.

T he next night I stood on a balcony high over Manhattan and looked into the dark null that was Long Island and sipped a Krug blanc de blanc from a Riedel tulip glass. The wine was too heavy for my tastes—for champagne, it felt almost lugubrious—but it was a touching gesture from a client who'd chosen us over Sotheby's to sell his world-class collection of Mayan art. Normally I liked this sort of party. The room was filled with people who appreciated what I do, people I knew quite well from a thousand little things that were in fact meaningful as hell, my loving sister's opinion notwithstanding. Normally I wouldn't be so critical of what was probably the most expensive champagne I'd ever have a chance to drink. But I'd accepted the glass with extravagant joy and then retreated to the balcony when the string quartet started to play and I just stared out into the night. At forty stories up, there was a breeze riffling around me and I turned away from Long Island, happy I was back in the city, happy I was at this party. I followed the ribbons of head-lights and taillights down past the hulk of the Empire State Build-ing and on into the dim forest of Lower Manhattan.

"May I?"

I looked over my shoulder. It was Alain in a tux.

"I didn't see you in there," I said.

"I'm late. May I intrude once more?" Haydn was flittering around his words.

"No intrusion," I said and he slid up beside me. We faced the city together.

"Last time . . ." he began.

"It wasn't you," I said. "I left because of someone else." I was surprised to be confiding this much in Alain.

"Ah yes. The man at the bar."

"The man at the bar. Did he speak to you?"

"No. Not at all. Once we'd each blundered in so obviously, we became quite perfect models of discretion."

"You were right," I said. "About my bidding for myself. He's the guy I outbid."

"A sore loser then? He came to see who had won."

"Something like that."

"So he must have thought . . ."

"It was you. Yes."

Alain turned sideways to face me. "I hope I didn't cause some complication."

By rights this should have sounded sincere. He'd even tried to make it more than words—he'd turned to me to show his earnestness. But there was a not quite repressed bubble in his voice—a ripple of animation beneath the surface—that struck me with the opposite meaning. He was quite pleased to think he might have caused a complication with this man. It felt like the Alain of my first impression—determined to be in control.

So I turned to face him and said, "I think it's time to talk about what I need to keep me at Nichols and Gray." It was the right move, to cut through the faux personal crap and remind him that if I was a valued asset, he still hadn't made an appropriate bid. But as soon as I said it, I realized the abrupt and aggressive change of subject could be taken as an admission that he'd caused a complication. Still, it was abrupt enough and aggressive enough to make him flinch, and I just focused on enjoying that.

He furrowed his brow and struggled to figure out what was going on between us. "Do you mean tonight? Here?"

"I mean before we go on with each other in some vaguely personal way."

He unfurrowed his brow and bowed ever so slightly to me. "You're quite right." I wanted this to seem patronizing, but it didn't. It felt respectful. I was about to interpret this impression but I suddenly grew weary of reading the little things.

"But not tonight," I said. "Not here."

"Good." He turned away. And even this struck me as a gesture of respect—he resumed the posture we'd been in before he began to piss me off.

"You're missing an expensive champagne," I said, squaring around to Lower Manhattan, as well.

"Yes? It's good?"

"I only said expensive. It's a bit heavy-handed for my taste."

I didn't consciously mean this as a further dig at him, but he breathed one faint humph that told me he'd taken it this way. I realized that I liked—very much—this man's ability to communicate with a woman in metaphors and indirections. And I realized that I disliked—very much—that this was one more bit of evidence he was gay.

He said, "So then I will avoid this champagne, no matter how expensive it is."

Had I ever known a man who was straight who could talk like this?

We looked at each other briefly.

I didn't think so.

I lifted the still half-full tulip glass of Krug Clos du Mesnil between us and then moved the glass out beyond the balcony and inverted it, dispatching the champagne into the night breeze.

I woke up in a sweat before daybreak that Monday morning, thinking, God please, no, I've only just turned forty, don't let this be a hot flash. Then I tried to convince myself that the air-conditioning had gone out. But I could hear it clearly, whistling through the vent. I felt the movement of the

air. Then I understood I'd been dreaming. Texas. I was in a sweat
over Texas. I couldn't remember the dream now, but I didn't
want to anyway. I turned on my back, threw off the sheet. I was
still hot. Daddy was looming at my side. Not a dream. A memory
now. I let myself think of him. We were walking in the smell of
cattle—straw and shit and slobber and the flanks fetid like after
a rain. More than the smells. The cattle were stirring in little
pens on both sides. My daddy was looking this way and that,
sizing them up, telling me what he was seeing, the good things.
Broad muzzle, he said. Short face, strong jaws, brisket trim and
neat, breast wide and full, rump long and wide and level, pin
bones wide apart. And I was beside him, moving with him, it
was just me and him. You've got a feeling for this, he said to
me. You'll understand. And I was so happy for these words that
I wanted, then, more than anything, for him to take my hand
as we walked. But he didn't. Instead, he said, "Keep up," and I
knew it was on me. I knew he didn't want me to take his hand,
he was teaching me to keep up, he trusted me to keep up. But
he'd touch Missy. He'd take Missy's hand for sure, I knew. Because she couldn't keep up, I'd tell myself. This wasn't her place.
Sitting in the stands now with the tight auction floor below. The
old black man moving around us, selling peanuts. The auctioneer rolling out the numbers.

I opened my eyes and I was in a bizarre little panic. Lying
here, I couldn't remember the numbers. A three-year-old Shorthorn cow had dashed into the circle and I couldn't even think
what it was worth. I couldn't hear any numbers from whenever this was. What would a fine breeding Shorthorn go for in
1972? Or even now? I had no idea. I was in a sweat again. I

dragged a forearm across my face. I was letting him down. How could I not know the value of a thing to be auctioned? I listened to the auctioneer, my daddy leaning forward beside me. "Thank you, one thousand is bid and do I hear eleven? Eleven, and twelve, who's for twelve, twelve, and now thirteen. Thirteen. Thirteen, and who'll do fourteen. Fourteen come fifteen. Fifteen now." And the words rolled out. I was still doubting the numbers. Was I just forcing those in?

We were standing at a fence line. Daddy was smoking. The free range was before us. Briefly he laid his palm on the top of my head. I touched the side seam of his jeans with the back of my forefinger. Lightly, so he wouldn't know. His hand lifted from me but I held still, pressing the back of my hand gently against his leg. The horizon was flat and far away. In between, our cattle posed, not moving. The sun was hot. I was sweating.

"Daddy," I said.

"Yes?"

"Nothing," I said. And this was true; there was nothing in particular. I just wanted to say his name.

Missy on his lap, her arms around him. "Little dumpling," he said. "Little moonpie."

"Little sheep-dip," I said. Mama's hand came from somewhere—from around the dinner table—and slapped my forearm. But this time, Daddy caught my eye and gave me a quick wink. At least I thought he did, though now he was ignoring me again. One more time, please, Daddy, please, so I'd know that what I saw was real. But Mama was going on about me eating my food and me keeping a civil tongue in my head and he wouldn't look at me again and Missy wouldn't climb down.

I sat up in my bed. I was drenched. I was getting old. Who the fuck in my position, knowing who I know, selling what I sell, would care what a goddam cow was worth?

I got out of bed. I stripped off my silk nightshirt on the way to the bathroom and I stepped into the shower and I turned on the water, cold at first, then I made it warmer, then warmer still until I grew calm again under water that was hot as a Texas noon.

After the shower, after dressing, after coffee and a bagel and experiencing the sunrise by watching a certain high strip of windows I could see over the rooftops from my kitchen—their glass changing from black to gray to white to the blurred yellow dazzle of reflected sun—after reading the *Times* and clipping the obituary of a banker whose estate would include, if my memory served correctly, a major collection of ancient Roman silver, I thought about Mama. I still hadn't returned her last call and so I went to my couch with the portable phone and sat and dialed, looking up at the Dalí Mary and Jesus, and he was remarkable, Dalí, in his restraint. He was in a sober mood with none of the surrealistic excess. There was only a mounding up of black strokes like straw, and only by easing into the image could you see the mother's face, without features, bending to a tiny child who then showed his eyes and an expressionless mouth. The phone rang a fourth time in Houston and I expected her answering machine, but her voice was abruptly there.

"Hello?" she said.

"Hello, Mama. It's me."

"Yes? Hello?" She was playing dumb, making me pay for not calling enough.

"It's Amy, Mama."

"Amy. I'm so glad. Are we being taped?"

"Taped?" Though she had never shown the slightest sign of dementia I instantly assumed she thought the FBI or CIA or someone was bugging our call.

"The gol-durn machine," she said. "I have to run to beat the fourth ring."

I was relieved. "I think you made it in time."

"My heart is palpitating."

"Relax, Mama. It's okay. The machine didn't answer."

"I hate machines."

"Not all of them."

"Your father liked machines."

"He liked cattle."

"He liked Lone Star Beer, too, but that's neither here nor there."

The conversation was already getting out of hand in a way that often happened between us. "Mama," I said, "hello. How are you?"

"Hello, Amy. How are you? I'm not so fine."

There was a pause.

I knew what she was waiting for. "Do you want me to ask?"

"What?"

"Why you're not so fine."

"Don't ask."

"Okay."

"My heart is still palpitating."

"You don't have to run to the phone. *Let* the machine answer it."

"Other times, too."

"Go to a doctor, Mama."

"I get lonely."

"You've got friends there, don't you?"

"Of course."

"Call them."

"It's so gol-durn hot."

"Turn the air-conditioning up, Mama. You don't have to keep it at seventy-eight. You've got plenty of money."

"Amy, you talk just like a man. I tell you I've got a problem and all you can do is offer a solution."

She waited a beat, but I had no answer for this.

Then she said, "Are you sure you're not lesbian, honey?"

"Mama."

"Not that I'd judge you."

"I'm not a lesbian. But even if I were, that's not the same as a being a man."

"Your father is dead."

Usually I could follow the eccentric associative leaps of her mind, but this one puzzled me. "I know, Mama."

"I'm all alone now."

"We could get you a place out here, Missy and I. You could get a nice place close to everyone."

"I'm a Texan."

"You're probably right about that."

"And so are you," she said.

"I don't think so anymore."

"You both are. You'll always be."

"Okay, Mama. Okay."

"I'm surrounded by your father's things."

I heard this as another reason she couldn't move. I was wrong.

"I want to get rid of them," she said.

"What?"

"He liked machines. I've got chain saws, electric carving knives, stereos and TVs galore. My garage door opens like the jaws of hell when the police use their radios in the neighborhood. I've got a Ford pickup and a Hummer and a Cadillac something-or-other beyond the nice little BMW that I use. Don't tell me I'm contradicting myself. I know that's a machine, but I can like my BMW."

"You can give most of that stuff away," I said.

"I need your help."

"Take the excess vehicles to a used-car lot. For the rest, just call one of your charities. You couldn't get more than garage-sale prices for it, anyway. "

"That's fine for the things I mentioned. But there are plenty of valuables, too. Things he collected. Jewelry he bought me. Furniture he chose. I want to get rid of it all. And I want some money for it"

I'd paid easy lip-service to Mama's hatred for Daddy. But in the face of a clear, avid expression of it, I found myself trembling faintly.

"I need your help with a lot of this," she said.

"I don't know."

"You won't help me?"

This was an intensely unpleasant prospect, but there was no excuse. "Of course I will," I said. "But are you sure?"

"I'm sure. You can come down, okay? Look it all over. I don't want to get hornswoggled."

"Okay, Mama. I just don't know when."

"As soon as possible, honey. There's a bull moose staring down from the wall at me right now. I'm tired of living in the middle of all this."

"You can get rid of the moose right now, Mama."

"You don't think it's valuable?"

"Only to Daddy."

"He's dead."

"I know."

"Then the moose is outahere."

The thought of going to Houston to evaluate my father's things rasped at me through a quiet Monday at work, and then on Tuesday morning there was a padded envelope, without stamps and without a routing slip, sitting in the center of my desk. In a bold hand, using what I recognized as a flexible-nib fountain pen—probably vintage—was my name "Amy Dickerson" in the center and a simple "Bouchard" in the return address spot. I called for Lydia, who appeared in my doorway and seemed hesitant to cross the threshold without permission.

"When did this arrive?" I asked, nodding to the envelope.

She clearly didn't know what I was talking about. I held it up.

"I've never seen it," Lydia said.

"Thanks."

"Honest," she said.

"I believe you. Thanks."

She disappeared and I sat down. I never locked my office. Alain had slipped in early this morning—or late last night—and placed this here himself.

I opened the envelope and inside was a cobalt blue Groupe Bouchard S.A. folder. In the folder was a thick, slick booklet on his corporation, a formal tender of stock options in the parent company, a salary offer that represented a fifty-percent raise, a commission proposal that gave me three extra points, an open-date airplane ticket to Paris, and a folded heavy-vellum note with the flexing nib shaping the words from thick downstrokes to delicate thin swoops and back again, the written equivalent, it felt, of Alain's expressively conversational hands.

Dear Amy Dickerson, I hope these figures make you wish to remain a part of Nichols and Gray. Since under this proposal you would, as you can see, own a part of my company, I invite you to come to Paris to visit the headquarters. You may do so at any time, though Arthur will be coming soon and perhaps you wish to accompany him. But first, shall we have a dinner before I leave NewYork? I promise not to be vaguely personal. Alain Bouchard.

I folded the note and put the whole packet together again, sliding it all back into the envelope, and then I laid it on the center of my desk where I'd found it, squaring up the sides so that it was perfectly horizontal there, and I stared at it. I thought of his little bow to me on the balcony Sunday night. I'd said no more bullshit—I hadn't used the exact word, but it felt like it; that was in my tone, certainly—and less than thirty-six hours later he'd made me an offer I was hardly inclined even to dicker about.

I rose from my chair and stood looking at the packet and I felt oddly affectless. I circled the desk and went out of my office and down the hall and straight into Arthur's office. He was in the sitting area beneath his corner windows, sipping coffee at one end of his silk brocade couch while Winona sat at the other end pointing a microcassette recorder in his direction. Arthur was composing a letter. He missed dictating to a secretary who hunched over a notepad taking shorthand. He'd acceded to modern technology enough to use a machine, but he still insisted on his assistant holding it while he talked.

"I'm sorry to interrupt," I said, though in fact I wasn't.

Arthur lifted a hand toward Winona to pause the recording and said, "It's all right, dear. We'll finish later."

Winona shrugged and rose and she slipped past me and Arthur patted the couch next to him. Though it shouldn't have been a gesture that appealed to me, I went to the spot he'd patted and sat and Arthur took my hand and gave it a little squeeze and in spite of myself I suddenly felt sweetly cozy.

Arthur leaned near me and said, low, "Did he make you a nice offer?"

"Didn't he tell you what it was?"

"Of course not. That's a private matter between the two of you." Arthur said this grandly, as if it were a statement of personal philosophy.

"You asked and he wouldn't say."

"In spite of my twisting his arm."

I smiled at Arthur's quick reversal. He squeezed my hand again.

"You know me so well, my dear."

"It's a pleasure," I said.

"So. Was he good to you?"

"He was."

"Very good?"

"Very good."

"Splendid then. Splendid." He sounded relieved. He also was assuming that a very good offer would necessarily lead me to stay. Hearing the assumption in his voice made me realize what this lingering affectlessness was all about. In fact, I *hadn't* decided I'd stay. I could read Arthur instantly but I suddenly was lagging way behind on myself.

But before I'd examine that, I wanted to know about the relief I'd heard. "Didn't you expect the offer to be good?"

"Yes. Of course."

"Very good?"

"Of course."

"Arthur."

"Well, perhaps I wasn't quite so sure. I told you he was a hard bargainer."

"What did he say about me?"

"Only the highest, sweetest things." Arthur took my hand again and looked me squarely in the eyes. I believed him.

"And how about you?" I said. "Was his offer to you a hard one?"

"Buying the company, perhaps that's a different matter."

"Does he want you to stay on?"

"He does."

"Good," I said, and I realized I'd worked up a potential little panic with the question. I wanted Arthur always to be around. This time I squeezed his hand, and I realized I was making the same assumption he did. "And will you stay?"

"What else is there?" he said and I couldn't figure out his tone.

I pressed on. "Do you mean you'd like an alternative but there's none?"

"I mean it's who I am."

"That doesn't quite answer my question," I said.

"Would I like an alternative me?"

He was right. That's what I was asking. But it wasn't about him. I said, "I can't imagine a different Arthur. Just tell Bouchard yes and let's get on with our work."

"That's the ticket," Arthur said, brightening.

I'd said *our* work. But it didn't feel like a decision. Still, I let it stand for now with him. And with myself. Another issue pressed itself on me. I said, "Arthur, I may need to go to . . ."

"Perhaps we can go together," he said. "Right after the Ravel auction."

"That's fine," I said. "I'd be happy to. But I wasn't talking about Paris."

"I'm sorry."

"No way for you to know. I was going to say Houston. My mother wants to auction my father's things. I'll need to take care of that."

Arthur, bless his heart, suddenly looked worried. "How very strange for you," he said. "Would you like me to get someone . . ."

"That's sweet of you, Arthur. But I think that would feel even stranger, somehow."

"Then go whenever you need to."

He took my hand. I leaned over and kissed him on the cheek.

When people begin to collect a new thing—even if they are experienced collectors of something else—they will often make a common mistake. I am particularly attentive to our frequent bidders, whose every crotchet is known to me, as they move to a new category, so that I can make use of this phenomenon. These collectors will, early on, buy items that later—after their tastes have undergone an inevitable process of refinement—seem too common or undistinguished for their collection. I call this a "mistake," but who's to say? It can also be seen as a necessary first step into a new world. It can be seen as that classic time of initial enthusiasm for a whole new category of the world's rich variety of objects, a time when even common things can be seen afresh and with delight. Which is why I can absolve myself of most of the guilt when I manipulate the hell out these people and move the typical middle-of-the-auction batch of mediocre stuff out the door for good prices. The sellers are happy, Nichols and Gray is happy, and the buyers, at least for a while, are happy.

As I walked back to my office after my little hand-squeezing session with Arthur, this whole process was on my mind. I realized that what I'd done in East Hampton was not simply to buy myself. I am not a one-time, single-item purchase. At the charity auction I had, in fact, begun to *collect* myself. I'd started by overpaying for a commonplace dinner in a restaurant with me, though it had a couple of features I'd not expected—a way of slowing down to eat, a rare moment of enjoying my own dinnertime company, an instructive encounter with a couple of men. Still, there were other items of Amyania—*many* items— yet to be acquired. Right at that moment, for instance, a pretty important one—vocation, profession, calling. Was there an alternative Amy Dickerson, one who was not an auctioneer?

Here was her office, however. I closed her door and sat down and swiveled her chair to face the terra-cotta lions. There had been an Amy Dickerson before Nichols and Gray. I was lanky then. Fresh Texas face. Something like that. I swirled my newly washed hair—given body and dazzle by Prell shampoo—for the viewers of half a dozen soap operas and the noontime news in fifty major local markets. Dressed in a Versace gown at the New York Auto Show, I lay draped across the hood of the last Yugo model to be sold in the United States, with bombs already falling in Croatia, and I sang—to the tune of "Camptown Races"—"You want to drive a stylish car, you go Yugo. You want to make your cash go far, you go Yugo, too. She can run all night, she can run all day, still you'll not fill up her tank, for Yugo we shout hooray."

It had occurred to me—I was, in fact, about to make a career change—that I could do a much better job of selling the idea of this car with my own words. Car buyers knew what a wimp the thing was. I'd go straight to the worst of what they were thinking. Sixty-two horsepower? Hell yes. That's plenty to get you where you're going, and when the shit once again hits the fan in the Middle East, you'll be happy you've got fewer mouths to feed under that hood. But I'd sung that goddam song a hundred times just as it was when I finally realized something had to be done about my life, and so instead of improving the sales pitch, I gave it quite a different spin, in order to turn in my resignation. One night with a pretty good crowd milling around I stood up straight and practically deep-throated my mike to sing, "Tito's dead and so's this car, bye-bye, Yugo. Without new parts you won't go far, oh the Yugo's dead. The gears are prone to strip, the gas tank catches fire, inside a year you'll fix this car, with gum and baling wire."

This ended my acting career, though it was clearly in the same state as the Yugo by then anyway. And a few years later I sold the most weirdly beautiful car in the world—one of only three ever known to exist—in a private auction in Darien. It was a 1938 Bugatti Type 57 Atlantic, created by Ettore Bugatti's son, Jean, who died the next year test-driving a LeMans racer and killed the company at the same moment by devastating Ettore, who in his grief found it in himself effectively to make bombs and torpedoes for Mussolini but failed utterly to make more cars. My Atlantic was midnight blue with great billowing front fenders and swooping lines and a low central fin starting at its radiator and splitting the wind along the hood and up the center of the angled windshield and over the sweet, tight curve of the roof and down a long, unmodulated slope through the back windows—which looked more to the heavens than the road behind—and down the trunk to the bottom of its bumperless tail. And I had half an hour in a room alone with this car and I draped myself over its hood and I sat in its suffocatingly small cabin and it smelled of leather and very old wood and I sold the hell out of it, to three dozen connoisseurs, and I made them see even more vividly what was there in that room with them, the beauty of it, the dark history of it, and they ran past the estimate and on and on and I gaveled it down at seven million dollars, even.

Why was I hesitating to accept the offer sitting behind me in the center of my desk and settle in to the rest of my professional life at Bouchard's Nichols and Gray? Was I thinking of going to some other house? There was only a handful of them in our league and they all operated more or less the same way, if anything somewhat more conservatively. I knew they'd probably try to tone down my podium style. If Bouchard and his company looked okay, there was no point in moving on. The lions before me yawned in boredom at all this thinking.

But my hesitation ran deeper. Was there a drastically different Amy that I should hunt down? I spun around in the chair and laid my hands on the desktop. Was there a fourth Bugatti Atlantic out there somewhere, tucked away in a fieldstone barn in a village in Tuscany? Original paint. American Beauty red.

For a few days I put aside any thoughts of a future beyond the imminent Music Manuscript and Vintage Instruments auction, and I made that dinner date with Alain for Saturday night. I spoke only with his secretary—he himself had dashed back to France for a couple of days—and when the time

came, a Lincoln Town Car arrived for me at the door of my
building. I answered the doorman's buzz and stopped for a
moment in the center of my apartment, caught by the vague
impulse to consider its silence. And then I went down the elevator and across the marble lobby and out the door and for some
reason I did not expect Alain to be inside the car. But the chauffeur opened the back door and bowed a little and I plunged
into the smell of seat leather and there Alain was, taking my
hand in both of his.

The door clicked shut and he said, "I'm so sorry to have
been away when you called."

He let go of my hand and I said, "I hope you had a good
trip."

"Ça va," he said.

We rolled away from the curb and the car was dim and
we made small talk for a few moments, but then we rode in a
silence that, surprisingly, felt entirely comfortable, with nothing to prove to each other, no impressions to cultivate, just
here we are in New York on a Saturday night. The lights of
the city splashed on Alain's face and washed away and splashed
again and he seemed much younger in the dark and he smelled
of something earthy, deep-woodsy, but very nice, patchouli
perhaps. I would have expected him to smell just slightly too
sweet.

He'd heard I liked sushi and so we ended up in the Village
at a place with a woman planted in a corner in a kimono, playing
a koto, and he told me of his regard for sumo wrestling, its tradi-
tions and its ritual and the psychological subtlety of the struggle,
the wrestlers waging a war of the eyes for a long while before the

actual clash, which itself, he said, was often quite wonderfully graceful. He made a joke with the Japanese waiter about the Ozeki-brand saki, saying it should be called Yokozuna saki, which, he explained to me after the waiter went away laughing, was actually a higher sumo rank than Ozeki. All of this, and we were through our gyoza and seaweed salads, before he finally said, "I trust you found the envelope of information."

"I did. Thanks." I knew he wanted me to answer questions that he was trying not to ask, but I said no more.

A platter of sushi, chosen specially by the chef, arrived in time to get us both off the hook. We focused on the sea urchin and the monk liver and things I could not name and had never eaten before and we prowled the ocean, Alain and I, taking in our fellow creatures raw, and all we spoke about was how good it was, how very good were these tastes in our mouths.

At last, over green tea ice cream and more saki, I said, "I don't mean to be coy."

He acted genuinely puzzled.

"About your offer," I said.

"I don't mean to pressure you."

"I appreciate that. It was nice just talking about food for a while."

"Yes," he said. For a moment he waited, and I could feel him trying to assess whether it was time now to talk about business. I gave him no further help, scraping my ice cream bowl with my spoon as if I couldn't bear to leave a single dollop behind.

Finally he said, "Do you have any questions for me? About the offer? Or perhaps the company, its goals?"

In fact, I found that I had no questions at all, though neither had I made a clear decision. My hesitation was beginning
to feel like a low-grade depression. I did say, "I look forward to
going to Paris."

"Yes. And of course, when Arthur and I have finished our
work, you would have a chance, whenever you wished, to be
in Paris—and London also, eventually. It's time for Nichols and
Gray to have European operations."

I realized that all through this, Alain's hands were still. They
lay on their heels, one on either side of the sushi serving block,
their fingers curled and slightly lifted, and though I knew them
to be important performers in Alain Bouchard's communica-
tion, there they lay. A reflection of what? Alain's seriousness of
purpose? Or his insincerity? Or was he depressed, as well?

My mind drifted back to the prospect of Nichols and Gray
finally having a Paris branch and London branch. "That's good
news," I said and I felt as brittle as that sounded.

"May I say one more thing?"

"Yes."

His hands finally lifted from the table, parted slightly,
turned, the palms facing each other—a papal gesture, actually,
which irritated me for some reason. "I want you to know my
relationship with regard to Nichols and Gray from this point
on." His hands came together, the fingers intertwining. "I have
a special fondness for this business, as I explained to you. So
I've been handling this transaction as a kind of . . ."

He hesitated, looking for a word, and his hands came apart,
turned palms up, the fingers gently closing as he finally caught
the one he wanted. "Self-indulgence," he said, and the hands

clasped each other again. "I do my own work at a far remove from the daily operations of things. Do you understand?" And his hands let go of each other and came outward, wanting to fall before me, I think, though the wooden-block serving tray that sat in front of Alain made that awkward.

"I understand what you're saying," I said, with the rest of the thought simply implied. I didn't understand why he was saying it.

He said, "I will not be your boss in any direct way. Even indirect. It will be as if I was in another line of business, in the exercise of my own, shall I say, *power,* by which I mean authority, certainly, but also any *personal* intimidation or influence I might have with an employee."

Through this, Alain's hands made a soft stirring motion in the air between us, and as this authoritative and, shall I say, *powerful* man suddenly and uncharacteristically struggled for words—perhaps even *because* of his struggle—I began to consider his hands more and more closely, seeing now the squarish shape of his nails, the thickness of his fingers—these were working hands, retired now, softened, capable of gentleness but still used to grasping a thing tightly, working hard—and then, as the men's hands I'd collected in my memory all do, Alain's hands struck me as *naked,* as intimate parts of him. I turned my eyes away.

"Do you see?" he asked.

"No," I said, and that was the truth.

"Ah," he said.

And we neither of us said anything more until the waiter had brought Alain the check and he'd paid it and we'd dith-

ered around with the last of the saki and with our napkins and
our water glasses and we finally looked at each other and smiled
politely and his hands were down again, exhausted, I think,
lying flat on the table very close to him, nearly sliding off out of
sight.

"So," he said at last. "What would you like now?"

"I don't know."

"To have another drink?"

"I've probably had enough."

"To say good night?"

I was indeed feeling suddenly very weary. "Would you
mind?"

"I am myself weirded out from the time zones."

"Weirded out? Where did you pick that up?"

"Arthur's secretary. Did I not use it correctly?"

"You did. Though perhaps not to describe jet lag."

"Jet lag. That's what I have."

"Then we should say good night." I suddenly felt disappointed.

"I'll take you home," he said.

And so we went out of the restaurant, and the Town Car
was waiting for us. Alain waved off the chauffeur and opened
the back door for me himself. I went in and Alain followed and
we rolled off again into the night.

"Thank you," I said at once. "The sushi was good."

"Yes," he said. "I will take you to a place in Paris."

I looked at him, touched by this Frenchman's first impulse
to cater to my Asian taste even in his beloved Paris. His face,

turned to me, was in darkness, but even as I looked, a light from the street flashed across his eyes.

I said, "In your city, I'll leave my New York tastes behind."

The light was gone but I could see his hand rise and move in a fast-rising and then slow-falling arc. Whatever I can do to make you happy, it said.

"Do you like my city already?" he asked softly.

"I do," I said.

"Do you *love* my city?" he said, even more softly.

"I do," I said. "I love Paris."

And then the darkness that was his face, his body, moved closer, as if he were sleep coming upon me, and I could smell the deep woods at night and I could feel his hand fall naked on my forearm, lightly, and his face came nearer and his lips touched mine, very gently, his lips touched mine and then, very briefly, they took my lower lip between them and tugged it sweetly and let go. He drew back as smoothly as he'd approached and I found I was holding my breath. Then I let the breath go in words, dreamy words, relieved words: "You're not gay."

Alain laughed as gently as the kiss.

I understood now why he'd flailed around for words about his not actually being my boss. He was trying to establish how it would be all right for us to become involved.

"I'm sorry to have waited so long to do this thing," he said. "If that's what gave you the impression . . ."

"I'm not that vain," I said.

"Perhaps I should not ask you then how I gave this impression."

"It wasn't you. You've done everything just fine."

"Yes?"

"Everything."

He laid his hand on mine. Just right. He kept it there and we said no more until we stopped in front of my apartment building. Also just right.

Now we faced each other and the chauffeur was getting out to attend to the door and my doorman was coming up too and it was not time to ask Alain to come up and still we did not speak. I simply turned my hand beneath his and our palms kissed and the door opened and I was out of the car and across the bright hardness of the lobby and I was rising in the elevator, alone, with the faint whir of the cable and the ping of the floor counter and I thought of him being here now, this Alain Bouchard, and suddenly I jump up on him and hook my legs around his hips and take his face in my two hands and kiss him some more and we make love in an elevator. And would that make me a hypocrite? Did this little fantasy subvert my recent self-possession? No. Alain and I had gone slow enough. We'd been to a restaurant. I'd even disliked him for a brief time. And it would be *my* act. And my actual, real-life act was not even to kiss him a second time, just to touch the palms of our hands.

The elevator stopped and the door opened and I moved along the hallway thinking he would one day soon be walking beside me in this very space and I squeezed this giddiness out of my head and I unlocked my door and went in and I leaned back against the door as it clicked shut. I would not get ahead of myself. There were still too many unknowns about this man.

But it was true that as I stepped into the middle of my apartment, the silence had a different quality, no longer being a thing unto itself, a thing without a beginning and promising no end, but a silence of caesura now—voices have just spoken and have paused and will begin again. I ran the tip of my tongue slowly along my lower lip.

And I found myself looking at the answering machine. A habit. Also by habit I touched the play button, as there was a red 1 announcing itself. And the voice in the room was Missy's, saying, "I need to see you. I'm divorcing Jeff."

S he wanted to come into the city and I met her the next morning at the lower-level information booth at Penn Station amid the smell of donuts and pee. She came up to me from behind, saying my name. I turned to her and I don't know who initiated it but we hugged, which we hadn't done in a long time.

"Where can we go?" she said.

"Inside or out?"

"I don't give a damn," she said. "Let's just walk, I guess."

We went up the escalator and out onto Seventh Avenue and it was a warm Sunday morning and I thought Missy would have wanted privacy for this, but she seemed not to notice anyone in the street. We just headed off uptown and she said, "Don't rub my face in this, okay?"

"Would you expect that from me?" I asked and I knew the answer at once. Of course she would expect that from me. We'd given each other little better for years.

She said, "It's bad enough I don't have anybody else to talk to about this."

It seemed a good sign, her giving me a hard time right off. She was ready to fight.

"Where are the girls?" I said.

"Oh, there are plenty of other-mom friends to give your kids to."

"Do they know? The girls, I mean."

"They know we've had a big stink and daddy's gone off on a trip. Do they know our lives are about to fall apart? No. Who ever knows that until it just happens?"

I pulled Missy back from plunging off the curb in front of traffic. "Pay attention," I said.

"It's a little late for that," she said.

"I mean the cars."

"Pay attention, my ass," she said.

I was still having to hold her back at the curb. She was utterly unaware of anything but what was jumping around in her head. This did *not* seem a good sign.

"Wait for the light," I said.

"Oh sure. That's *easy* to say."

"I'm talking about the fucking traffic, Missy. Wake up."

She looked at me squarely. "Nobody waits for the fucking light in New York City."

"As much as I like you talking dirty, little sister, I want you to settle down for a few minutes and tell me what happened. Can you do that?"

She looked first at the light, which was still telling us not to walk, and then east on 33rd, and she said, "See? We're good."

She shook off my hand and bulled on into the intersection and she was right this time, we had a few beats before another gaggle of cars, plenty of time by New York standards, and we were across and setting a brisk pace up Seventh.

The energy of her anger, the little signs I'd obviously misread at our recent dinner, the abruptness of all this, suggested that another woman was the problem. But Missy wasn't talking for the moment and I knew enough to let it go. After a block of power-walking I did say, "I'm sorry you can't come to me without fearing I'd give you a hard time."

"Yeah, well," she said, as if that were a complete thought.

"If you've got to end your marriage the only thing I feel is sorry. That's all."

"Mama's gonna shit a brick."

Ass, fuck, and shit, all coming from Missy's mouth within a few minutes of each other—if crisis brings out the hidden self in us, I was very pleased to meet my sister at last. Not that I dared compliment her at that particular moment. "Don't worry," I said. "Mama will blame me for everything."

"I don't care."

I didn't know if she meant about the blame or the brick.

"Do you?" she said.

"Care if she blames me?"

"Care who she blames."

"No."

"It's *his* fault anyway."

"Are you ready to tell me?"

She plowed across another intersection, just ahead of a honking cab.

But she stayed silent as we strode on. I thought of our last private conversation in Sea Cliff, watching the harbor. You do it all for the kids, she'd said.

"Well, for one thing, he's seeing somebody," Missy said.

I looked at her. Her walk slowed abruptly. The blunt talk had vanished. *Seeing somebody.* All my life I'd hated her prissiness. Now it just seemed pitiable. I wanted her to curse again. "Are you sure?" I said.

"Yes. And when I told him to get out, he went straight to her. You know? I called—I found some things written, I got her number—I actually got up the nerve to call her and he answered."

"You did the right thing," I said, softly.

"And it's *his* goddam couch."

"I noticed that."

"The TV's an eyesore and it cost way too much. But can we just order Chinese for dinner on the spur of the moment instead of having to anticipate it by six hours so we can get the cheap lunch specials and then heat them up later? No way."

"No fucking way," I coached.

"No fucking way," Missy said.

"Thata girl," I said.

But it was her last curse of the day. Missy dipped again and again into the box of odds and ends that held the collection of her husband—the grinding of his teeth in the night, discourses on portfolio management over dinner, the meticulous gathering of the crumbs at the bottoms of cereal boxes for a "free breakfast," eight-percent tips in restaurants because it's still better than the prime rate, the unilateral decorating touches—it was a grubby batch of stuff indeed and she lost her edge. And even when she circled back around to the "someone"—who had a sexy voice and a Queens telephone exchange—she couldn't work herself up. Instead, she wept. We sat in the back corner in a deli off Times Square and she wept quietly for a long while and I patted her hand and I tried to reassure her that divorce was okay. I asked her if she needed help finding a lawyer and she said Sea Cliff was full of them. I asked if I could do anything to help with the girls and she said maybe.

Then we walked back to Penn Station and I went down to the platform with her and waited until her train was sliding into the station. She squared around to face me. "Thanks," she said. Her eyes were puffy and weary but they tried to hold still on mine.

"I wish there was more I could do," I said. Then I thought of something. "Would you like me to tell Mama for you?"

"I'd be eternally grateful," she said.

I was appalled at how fast she accepted. Though the offer was sincere, I'd hoped she'd decline.

"I just can't face her right now," Missy said.

"But you want me to go ahead and tell her right away?" I said, and I regretted it at once.

The train doors opened and Missy looked in. Though she'd stopped cursing, not once had she questioned the finality of her husband's act.

"I'll do it tonight," I said.

Missy's eyes were on mine once more. "Why should we bring her into it at this point?" she said.

I willed myself to say the right thing now. "Because you're going to divorce this man. It's best for you and it's best for the girls. You can't teach them to let a man get away with this, can you? And after she beats up on me, Mama will be there for you."

Missy nodded and this seemed to be the moment for another hug. But in spite of some wiggling of the shoulders it didn't look like it was going to happen.

"Go on to your girls now," I said. "I'll take care of Houston."

We did an end-of-weekly-lunch bend from the waist and buss on the cheek, and Missy disappeared into the train.

I went along the platform and up the stairs and I thought not of Missy and her broken marriage, not of Mama and her unhappy marriage, I thought of Amy and Alain. I'd been a good sister all morning. But now I thought how—contrary to Missy's chronic self-righteousness about our respective lifestyles—it'd been me who'd always done things right. Look at the story of Amy and Alain. Here, Missy my sister, let me put the palm of my hand on the back of your head and press you down into the mess you've made doing things just so.

S unday seemed like a good time for Mama to get a dose of the truth. And I wanted to get this over with. So as soon as I got back to my apartment I curled up on my couch and dialed Houston. Mama answered on the first ring.

"You were sitting by the phone," I said.

"Hello? Who is this?" Mama said, feigning ignorance. She didn't like me simply to start up a phone conversation without a certain ritual of courtesies.

"You know my voice, Mama."

"Hello? Who's speaking please?"

"Cut it out, Mama."

"Can't we just do this right once in a while?" she said.

"Mama."

"Remember, this is Texas you're calling."

"Okay, Mama. Hello. This is Amy Dickerson your eldest daughter calling."

"No need to get snippety."

"Would you like me to hang up and call again and we'll do this the Texas way?"

"Is that a serious offer?"

I thought about that a moment. "Yes."

"Then no. We've gone this far, let's just keep on going."

"Things sound like they're getting to you, Mama."

"They are."

I thought about calling back later. This was not the way to tell her about Missy, after this kind of start. But before I could make a decision, she was crying. And it wasn't one of her exaggerated-for-effect Texas sob shows. Her crying was rather quiet, stuttery, almost repressed. In short, it sounded real.

I made my voice as gentle as I could make it. "Mama, what is it?"

"All his stuff is driving me crazy. I've got to move on, honey."

"Okay," I said. "I'll see if I can get down there tomorrow. You'll feel better when it's all tagged."

"I'm sorry about . . . you know."

I didn't know. "Sorry?"

"About making you say who you are. I know your voice."

"I know you do."

"You'll always be my little girl."

"Not for the rest of this week," I said. "I'm your auctioneer."

She was silent for a moment, weighing her desire for emotional leverage with me against her desire to get rid of Daddy from her life. Daddy won. "I can live with that," she said.

I was careful to give her a courteous close and then pushed the phone disconnect button, and though I'd committed to doing one unpleasant thing, I'd deferred another. It was better to tell her about Missy face to face anyway.

I stretched out on the couch, wanting to doze, and as soon as my legs moved I wanted Alain. I got up on my knees so I could see the answering machine, though I'd checked it when I got in, and there were still no messages, and I lay back down again. I didn't want to start second-guessing last night, but questions naturally arose. Did I do enough to let him know the kiss was right? Had he reconsidered the act for himself?

I looked to the clock over my fireplace. It was a gilt-bronze Louis XVI mantel clock, but it didn't make a sound. I'd gotten it cheap because the insides were hopeless and I'd had a quartz movement put in and my clients would be appalled at that but it kept better time than anything they owned in a pristine state.

It wasn't even noon. I had no reason to panic. I lay back. I was sleepy. I drew my arms to my chest and held in them that sweet, transitory emptiness that sometimes comes at the cusp of a love affair. A man you want exists in the world and you've not yet held him but you will and so you hold the emptiness for a time and it is precious in its nascence.

And the phone rang. I sat up. It was past one. The phone rang again and it was at my feet and I found it in the pillows and answered. "Yes?"

"I waited to call only because I imagined you'd be sleeping."

It was Alain.

"I was."

"Just now?"

"Yes."

"I'm sorry," he said.

"It was the best way to wait for this call."

"For me, it was not to sleep."

"All night?"

He hesitated. "I exaggerate."

I laughed. "I'm glad to hear you admit it. I don't want any sap between us."

"Sap?"

"Too sweet. Too cute. We should have no sentimentality."

"Good. But *sentiment,* yes?"

"Sentiment, yes."

"Then I will say to you that the kiss was splendid. For you, as well?"

"It was splendid."

"Good." He sounded relieved.

"We can do that again," I said.

"Very soon. But I have a meeting with Grumman. For one of my other businesses. I leave this afternoon and I'll be on the Long Island until Tuesday."

"I have to go to Houston," I said. "I won't be back until the end of the week, I'm afraid."

"This will be a test of our no-sentimentality rule," he said.

"Oh fuck that," I said. "Let's be sentimental."

"Very well. I will not sleep at all until we kiss again."

"Good." I tried to think of a sentimental thing to say. I couldn't. Finally I came up with "I won't kiss any man until I kiss you."

"Is that sentimental?"

"No."

"I'm feeling a little bit vulnerable now," he said.

"All right . . . The memory of our one kiss is worth more than all the other kisses of my life."

"Much better. I will carry that thought through my sleepless nights."

"Au revoir, Alain." And *this* felt legitimately sentimental, speaking French to him. I was from Texas.

"Bon voyage," he said.

The first word spoken from the moon was "Houston." I was proud of that as a girl of eight. As troubling as this trip was, when my plane came in over the piney woods north of the city I watched the familiar crawl of green below and felt a little rustle of pleasure to be back. I liked this city. I liked its cranks and mavericks and its unzoned sprawl and its nighttime landscape of lights and smoke out east through Channelview and beyond and I liked its salt marshes and bayous and its summers as hot as Cairo's and I liked its high-rise sculpture—especially that—a dozen or more of the most stunningly beautiful skyscrapers in the world. I rented a Sebring convertible at the airport and turned south on Highway 59, which was torn up like it always seemed to be, and I put the top down in spite of the slow traffic and the late afternoon heat, and I popped in a Dixie Chicks tape and off in the distance the skyline rose from absolute flatness into the subtropical haze.

I drove on and was happy when the traffic eased and I could get up some speed and let the hot wind blow my hair and I sang along with the Dixie Chicks about wide-open spaces and I thought of that hot Sunday afternoon when our city was hailed from the moon. My daddy jumped up and saluted the TV even though he'd been grumbling that it wasn't a man from Texas who'd be the first to set foot there—he's from goddam Ohio, Daddy said more than once about Neil Armstrong, I've been to Ohio and the sun doesn't even shine there for months at a time—and Missy'd gotten bored long ago and wasn't even in the room. This was my time at the center of things, though I was sharing it with the little overstuffed figure in black and white on the TV screen. But I still felt I was at the center because almost at once Daddy looked around for me and I jumped up beside him and he put his hand on the top of my head and he said, "There we are, Amy, out there in space. You and me and the whole world." And I thought, You and me. Yes. But not the whole world. It's just you and me. I reached up and put my hand on top of his. I'd do something important someday too, I thought. I could be the first person to raise cattle on the moon.

Now I was on I-10 and curving around Houston's wonderful big buildings and I loved the Philip Johnsons the most, of course, the red granite Bank of America Center with its three vast serrated gables and its Gothic spiky finials and then Pennzoil Place crouching nearby, its twin glass trapezoids barely separated, bronze and slick, shifting as I passed, seeming to touch, seeming to become one, parting again, and the other buildings, as well, a muted gray Pei now called the Chase Tower, the curved blue glass prow of the Enron Building, and out ahead, away from downtown, the great solitary lift of the Williams Tower, another Johnson, with a pyramid on top, an art deco homage in glass to the Chrysler Building and the Empire State, and this building used to be the Transco Tower, and the Bank of America Center used to be the NationsBank Center and before that the Republic Bank, and I gritted my teeth in envy. Of course, these great and lovely objects were bought and sold in a different way, but still I ached to auction them, to put Philip Johnson's eight-hundred-foot late-twentieth-century Gothic monument before a group of those who loved it as much as I and to articulate our shared passion and urge them on and on to express their regard, to bid for it, more and more, to proclaim the value of this wonderful thing.

I went down Shepherd and into River Oaks and along to our gated street and now my feelings about Houston began to grow more complex, moving under the canopy of oaks and elms through the landscape of my childhood, and I stopped at last in front of our house, and it struck me, looking at its long front veranda and its onion-domed tower and its cedar fish-scale shingles, how Missy had moved seventeen hundred miles away from Houston and then found her own version of our childhood home, though hers at least was authentically from the nineteenth century and this one was built by some oil magnet in a burst of nostalgia in the early twenties.

I pushed the button and waited for the car's top to come up from behind me and then put me in its shadow, and I secured it tight and I sat for a time in the car and I didn't want to go in. But Mama appeared on the front porch and she waved and I sucked it up and got out. "Hello, Mama," I called, moving to the trunk, my voice sounding small and muffled among the trees and the wide lawns, a thing that made me feel like I was still a child.

"I'm so glad you're here," she called in return, staying on the porch, waiting for me to come to her.

Which I did, rolling my suitcase, and I went up the steps and we kissed on the cheek. "Missy's getting a divorce," I said.

I hadn't meant to spring the news on her that abruptly. I regretted it at once but she didn't react the way I'd expected. I thought for sure I was in for a long session of having to both speak for Missy and defend myself for my malign influence on my little sister, meanwhile plucking Kleenex for Mama to sop up her tears. But instead, Mama went steely hard and simply said, "What is it. Another woman?"

"Yes."

"Where's Missy?"

"Probably at home."

And with that, Mama flew off into the house.

I stood on the porch for a few moments more with the clear conviction that I'd overlooked something important. I thought

I knew my mother well enough to accurately predict her behavior in a family crisis. Obviously not. What I did know for sure, however, were the smells of this porch—cedar and damp wood and faint whiffs of rust and car exhaust. They reassured me. I picked up my bag and stepped inside.

The house was dim—it had always been dim, the Queen Anne windows smallish, really, and each one covered with heavy dark drapes—and I looked around trying to put on my professional persona, trying simply to see the objects. Usually when major things in a house don't go together, you call it eclectic. But here, now, my impression was of schizophrenia. Even in the staircase hall where I stood. I hadn't recognized it before, but there were my mother's objects and my father's objects, side by side, distinct and unassimilated. A tulipwood marquetry console table against the wall, and hanging over it a mirror framed in scab-red mahogany carved full of dragons. A John Ellicott grandfather clock with applied color engravings of drastic biblical events—Adam and Eve slinking out of the garden, Moses parting the Red Sea, Jesus ascending into heaven—and nearby, hanging over the doorway to the parlor, a great rack of Brahma bull horns. The clock was ticking loudly and Mama's voice was coming from the back of the house, talking emphatically into a phone. "Missy . . . Missy . . . Stop crying and listen to me now," she was saying.

As surprised as I was by how Mama was reacting to all this, I had no energy at the moment for figuring it out. I shut off her voice, left my bag by the door, and moved beneath the horns and into the parlor. There hung Daddy.

Almost life-sized. Over the fireplace. He'd gone to New York sometime in the early eighties—six or eight trips, maybe more—to sit for his portrait. Stand, rather. The painting was meticulously representational, posing him full length with one arm akimbo, like an eighteenth-century duke. He wore cowboy boots with the brass tips glinting at the toes, faded jeans, a denim shirt buttoned at the throat with a black bolo tie, and his ten-gallon hat sat on a table next to him. He'd gone out there thinking to hire Leroy Neiman or Peter Max, but he decided that to be au courant meant to let go of center stage. He didn't want the portrait to be about the artist's techniques but about him. Fair enough. So he found a relatively unknown hyperrealist with a sense of humor and this painting certainly put Daddy at center stage. His sandy hair, barely going white at the sideburns and the eyebrows, was slicked back, and his wideset dark eyes were fixed on the viewer, and his square chin was faintly stubbled and cleft like Cary Grant's. It was Daddy there, no doubt about it.

I could still hear Mama's voice from the other room, though it was just a cajoling murmur now, not words, but it made me wonder why this portrait still hung here. Of course, she'd lived with the moose head till I'd given her a reason to dispose of it. But Daddy himself, I figured she'd have at least taken it down and stuck it away somewhere.

I returned Daddy's gaze for a moment and then tried to look away. It wasn't easy. I felt my eyes filling with tears and I couldn't let go. He hadn't been dead for all that long, after all. I remembered standing in this room—when? a few years ago, after I'd gotten going at Nichols and Gray, after Missy'd had Maggie but before Molly—Missy maybe was even pregnant, at the time—yes, I'd looked over to the window seat and Missy was there, beginning to show, her hand on her belly. It was Christmas. The first one in some years when we'd all been together. Daddy was quizzing me about my work. I was on Mama's Queen Anne walnut settee and Daddy was in his wing-back pony-skin chair. I'd long ago disappointed him. I'd finally found some people outside the family to make over me for how cute I was and how pretty and I'd collected enough of those responses in my head that I finally believed it and so I went east and I was pretty enough to want to make something of that and I put on other people's clothes for pay and I swung my newly washed hair for the cameras and I took on other people's names and lives on summer-stock stages and that was all a great mystery to Daddy.

I turned my eyes to the settee now and it looked the same as it always had, upholstered in pink-flowered brocade. When I'd sat there that Christmas, I'd already come to essentially the same conclusion as he. Those things I'd been doing were a frivolous waste of my life. So he was asking me about being an auctioneer, and pretty quickly he started to like it, I think. I took you to your first auction, he said. Yes you did, I said. I remember that, I said. Missy gave me a dark look from the window.

I blinked and shook off this memory. I was still staring at the settee. At least Daddy's eyes had let me go. I deliberately avoided looking at the portrait again. But I didn't let Daddy himself go. His den was through a door just ahead of me. I stepped forward. This was where I'd do most of my work this week. I touched the porcelain doorknob and hesitated. I was never allowed—none of us was allowed—to open this door without his express invitation. It was hard now to turn the damn thing. He was dead, I reminded myself. He died. He said at the end of his inquisition that Christmas, "This sounds like a step in the right direction," and that was his attitude for a few more years and that was fine with me, that was enough, and then he died.

I turned the knob and the door yielded and I stepped in and it was dark. The drapes were drawn—all the heavy drapes in this house were his, I think—he would ride a horse in the Texas sun, move among his cattle, visit his wildcat sites, all in the hot sun, and his hat would grow black around the band with his sweat, but in this house he wanted only darkness and little puddles of lamplight—and the air in the room was heavy with the smell of leather and old pipe smoke and books and gun oil. I moved to the massive desk in the center of the room and groped around and found the lamp. I pulled the chain and cut a swath in the darkness with light the color of cow piss.

The desktop had some scattered copies of *The Cattleman* and business papers and a phone book and a coffee cup. A little chill prickled along my scalp. He'd simply stepped away for a moment and was about to stride through the door and catch me in this place where I wasn't supposed to be. I turned. The door was closed. The room was still. I could no longer hear Mama's voice. I was an auctioneer. I was in this house to place a value on the objects I would sell. On one wall was a massive glass case full of vintage pistols and rifles and shotguns. Those were of value. Behind me was a wall of bookshelves. Daddy had a pretty sophisticated taste for old books. Good. Things to sell. A display case of miscellaneous objects—I remembered some pre-Columbian art in there. Other things. Some old pocket watches he was proud of. I thought of Alain's words about the collector—I own this thing, therefore I am—and I felt that chill again, as if Daddy had just put his hand on the top of my head. He didn't stride through the door because he'd never left. I was standing here in the center of him.

Which was not where I wanted to be at that moment. So I left his den and got my suitcase and Mama was going on and on with Missy and I went upstairs. I'd long ago accepted—indeed, embraced—the disappearance of our childhood rooms. Mine was Mama's sewing and house-hold accounts room, with almost none of my childhood furni-ture left. I'd have been hard-pressed to even pick the items out. Missy's room was the guest room, and that's where I went now. There was a brass bed and chintz curtains and it was all Mama. Missy, I knew, from a few unguarded words at some lunch or other, had been hurt by these transformations, but it seemed to me one of the few clearly healthy parent-child actions Mama had taken during our adulthoods.

I unpacked and came back downstairs and the two of them were still talking. I hesitated in the front hall. I could go out on the porch—that was the most obvious choice—but I had to get ready to do what I was here to do, so I stepped into the parlor once more and approached Daddy's pony-skin chair. I didn't think I'd ever sat in this chair before. Indeed, I couldn't remember *anyone* but Daddy sitting in it. I took a deep breath and I turned around and eased the backs of my thighs up against the chair and I was nervous as hell about this, but I made myself sit down. And now I was bareback on this pony and it was running fast and after a moment I let myself look over my shoulder to the left and above the fireplace and I nodded faintly to my father. He had no choice, of course, but his face had not altered. He was letting me sit in his place.

I waited without letting myself hear any of Mama's words. I know how I sound to myself sometimes. Much of the time, when it comes to my sister, I'm petty and jealous and stuck in a past that I should have left behind long ago. Oddly, at that moment, sitting in Daddy's chair, it was the very echo of the past—this room; the familiar, hectoring rise and fall of my mother's voice; the ticking of the clock—that made me regret the last chilly peck on the cheek with Missy on Sunday morning. I should have hugged her on the train platform. She'd even said "fuck." I smiled now, sitting in this chair, at the thought of Missy cursing. Daddy would—as Missy said of Mama—shit a brick if he'd heard his little googoopoo speak those words. I should have said, when our bodies returned to our stiff, minimal-contact posture, "Fuck this, Missy, let's hug." She needed that a hell of a lot more than what she was getting from Mama at the moment. Or what she got from Daddy, for that matter. Neither of us chose to have him shape us the way he did.

Still, I could not imagine Missy having anything like the thought I'd just had. However it was that she'd ended up this way, she was as unremitting in her criticism of me as Mama. She just used irony and indirection instead of full-frontal nagging and cajoling, which was why I could still keep my lunch dates with her and why I was starting to get very restless sitting here within earshot of even the mere tone of my mother's voice.

But then it stopped abruptly, the phone conversation. And soon after, Mama was standing in the doorway to the parlor surprisingly dry-eyed and with a faint look of astonishment on her face. I knew why. I was in his chair. He was looking down on both of us. I didn't move.

"How is she?" I asked.

Mama rolled her shoulders and came in. She sat on the far end of the settee. "She's confused."

"You told her to stay in the marriage," I said, keeping my voice flat, without judgment.

Mama shot me a hard look. Of course she had. And of course she knew I'd advised the opposite.

Mama eased off the look and glanced briefly beyond me— to Daddy, I knew—and then she looked away altogether, out the trapezium of bared window where the drapes had been wedged back as far as they would go. "I said some things." Her voice was low.

"I'm sure you did." I tried not to sound sarcastic, but I'm afraid I did.

"Not what you think," she said.

I waited. If she intended to repeat the things to me, she would. After a long moment, though, I got the feeling she was waiting, too. She wanted me to ask. I was curious, of course. But I wasn't going to ask. If she and Missy had a thing between them that she and I did not, she was going to have to offer it of her own free will.

Finally, Mama said, "Are you tired?"

"Of what?"

"From the trip."

"A little."

"What do you want to do?"

So that was that. She was content to keep me on the outside. At least I was motivated now to get the work done and get out of here.

"Lie down?" she prompted.

"No. You say you want everything of his to go?"

"Everything," she said, shaking off the little funk her voice had been in.

"I notice you haven't offered for me to take what I want."

"It hadn't occurred to me."

"Does Missy want anything?"

"I didn't offer to her, either."

"Are you now?"

Mama thought for a moment. "Is it up to me?"

"I'd say so."

"Then no. Sell it all."

"Okay."

She seemed suddenly to hear how she sounded. She said, "If there is anything . . ."

"I doubt if there will be. But thanks."

Mama nodded once and looked at the little bit of daylight she could let into the room.

"How about the drapes?" I asked.

She looked at me and smiled. "They're worthless."

"But they're his, aren't they?"

She shot them the same hard look I'd gotten a few moments ago. "You're right," she said. "They'll follow the moose."

And so it began. All that day and night and through the next day and night, as well, Mama and I hardly saw each other. When we did, there was only small talk, which we'd never done all that well together. But she seemed preoccupied. Whatever it was, I was grateful for it, because she did not speak of Missy's problem and she did not speak of what she saw as my problems and we put up an almost placid front for each other.

And there were, of course, Daddy's *things*. I made mostly lots of like items—with as much in them as I could get away with. But there were some special things, too. A Colt 1851 Navy-model revolver with figured walnut grips, an eighteen-karat-gold open-faced quarter-repeater pocket watch, a late-classic pre-Columbian Veracruz ceramic figurine of a woman with large, naked breasts. I found this woman in the deep shadows of a book shelf and I held her for a time, wondering how often Daddy looked at her. I sat her in the center of the desk and made my notes and it was late on my second day and I leaned back in the chair and dug my knuckles into my eyes to clear them.

I was weary. It was night. I thought of Alain, his arms around me in my drowsiness, but then that thought gave way to his hands. I held before me a vivid image of his right hand.

It lay on his knee, his leg crossed—I didn't remember where the image was from; perhaps the knee was simply a velvet display case I myself was supplying—I watched the hand, and the fingers were slightly curved, enough that the puckering at the knuckles had begun to smooth. I was happy for having his hands. I would kiss his knuckles someday. I thought to call him, but it was too soon for us to be doing that. We'd had a sweet good-bye on the phone and the next call should be to make the plan to bring us together.

I swiveled the chair once more to the bookshelves behind me. I'd found a fine leather set of *A History of the Pacific States of North America,* and the two volumes that included Texas were clearly more worn than the others. I knew it had been Daddy who'd done that. He kept care of his books, but he would read them. Driving the value down, of course, though I did not feel the slightest twinge of regret, as I can with other auction objects that need not be handled to be fully appreciated. I was good at bullying buyers into taking a book with the patina of use it deserved. He also had a nice Morocco-bound mid-seventeenth-century Calvinist King James printed in Amsterdam with annotations from the Geneva Bible, and a Civil War history of the Texas Volunteer Division, privately printed in 1869, written by an enlisted man, and a first edition of Frederick Douglass's *My Bondage and My Freedom,* this one clearly read many times and not just by my father, but the cloth covers were still whole and the pages were tight.

My eyes fell now to a lower shelf with oversized books laid sideways. A large volume I'd noticed and wondered about there finally moved me to lean to it and pull it out. As I'd suspected, it wasn't a published book at all but an especially fine leather album with heavy black photo pages. I moved the naked pre-Columbian lady well to the side and laid the album on the desktop, expecting family photos, I suppose, though having been in my professional groove for a couple of days, I may not have expected anything at all. I lifted open the cover, and there was Maidie, tipped in to the page in a monochromatic eight by ten. She was Daddy's first breeding cow. She was standing in a stock pen, her face turned languidly to the camera, and though her image had blurred from having been blown up from a Brownie-box photo, her large, dark eyes were clear and deep and sweet. I'd heard about Maidie. And on the next page was Ned, Daddy's first stud bull. And the facing page had smaller images of cows, four of them, and each was named and dated in Daddy's back-slanted hand, and I turned another page and another and it went on and on and they were all Daddy's special cattle, each one held here forever.

I closed the album. I heard him on the phone.

Where was I? Not at the office. I must have been at home. Yes, he woke me up. It was two or three, New York time. I answered the phone by my bed and my first thought was that he was gone. It was Mama calling to tell me he was dead. But it was Daddy's voice. He probably was sitting at this very desk, in this very chair. I looked now at the phone. His hand had reached out to that phone and picked it up and perhaps Maidie was looking at him from his desktop, though she was already long dead. He was sleepless and he was weak from the chemo, but his voice was firm.

"Amy, it's me."

"Daddy, are you all right?"

"All right?"

"Okay. I guess I meant, Are you *alive*."

"This is not a ghost calling you."

"I withdraw the question. It's late. I was sleeping."

"I'm sorry to wake you up," he said.

"You know I'm not complaining. If we're going to talk Texas-blunt, then don't pull the hurt feelings over nothing."

"You're right. And it *is* time to be blunt. I'm going to sell off the rest of the cattle, Amy. The whole ranch. I can't keep it up."

He fell silent and I waited. For a question. A plea for help. Something. But he wasn't saying any more. "Okay," I said.

"*Is* it okay?"

I finally figured out what he'd been waiting for. "You want me to stop you."

"I'm dying, honey. I can't keep doing this."

"You want me to say, It's time I quit all this meaningless stuff, I'm coming home and taking over the cattle business."

There was a long silence between us. Then he said, "I know you can't do that."

"It's what you always wanted," I said. "I understand that. I'm sorry."

"I didn't call to lay guilt on you," he said. "I guess . . . It's just that you were the only one who understood what I saw in them."

My breath caught at this, my eyes filled. I worked hard to keep my voice steady and I said, "I did, Daddy. You know I understood."

I laid my hand now on the cover of the album.

"Would you like to do the auction?" he'd said.

It was then that the tears spilled over, though his gesture was not a sentimental one, I knew, not even a gesture of genuine acceptance of the life I'd chosen for myself. The sudden brittle edge in his voice betrayed him. And I knew his ways. For the irony of it, yes, I wanted to auction off his cattle. But if I agreed, he'd figure to win either way. I'd get down there and in the midst of things, having to do the act myself, I'd see the light and I'd not go through with it. I'd stay and do what he'd always wanted. Either that, or he'd be able to hold my heartlessness against me. Not only was I making him sell off his dream for both of us, I was willing to hammer down the gavel with my own hand.

So I wiped the tears off my face hard and I said, "I can't, Daddy. I'm way too busy here. I'm their star." And that was true.

"You were always my star, too," Daddy said, and that wasn't true. I was surprised at his sudden plunge into bathos. But he was dying, after all. Maybe *no* declaration of attachment to things was sentimental if you were fucking dying.

Then he said, "I'm sorry we won't be able to ride the fence line together again."

He was pouring it on. I squeezed my eyes shut with my fingers.

And now, sitting at his desk, with him dead for more than a year, I consciously disconnected this memory. I pressed at my eyes, but from weariness. And I thought of a saddle. Just before he got sick, Daddy'd bought me a custom half-seat saddle from a maker out in New Mexico, built on an 1868 H.Y.A. Slick

Fork tree. It was a beautiful thing and I bet it would have been as comfortable as Missy's recliner, with a flat seat and a California twist in the stirrup leathers, which were bound with latigo lace. He probably spent close to three thousand dollars for the thing. I never even sat on it. What could I do with it? He gave it to me for Christmas when my auctioneer career was in full flight, and of course it wasn't meant to go to New York with me. I hadn't ridden in years. It was meant to sit in Houston and beckon me to return, to come back and ride the fence line with him like I'd done as a girl.

"You're going to beat this thing," I'd said to him that early dark morning when he'd called me.

"You know I'm not," he replied.

He left me with nothing more to say.

The phone rang and I woke. I sat up and fumbled to the night table, which wasn't there. I brushed metal with the back of my hand, grasped at it—the brass headboard. There was no phone. I listened. No sound. I lay back down. It was Daddy calling. I wondered: if I'd answered in my dream, instead of forcing reality upon the sound, what would he have said? I closed my eyes and invited the dream to return. But my head was full of *thoughts* now, no longer phones and voices and a saddle redolent of new leather. Where *was* that saddle? I'd not taken it with me, of course, though I'd slept with it in this very room for a night. Missy wasn't there, that Christmas, so Daddy'd been free to give me something he wouldn't know how to match for her. What did he do with the saddle after I left it behind?

Was it around this house? Did it get sold off with the cattle and the horses and the ranch?

I threw back the sheet and swung my legs over the side of the bed. They dangled there, not reaching the floor, which freaked me out a little bit. I'd shrunk back into my seven-year-old self. But it was nothing new. Mama'd put this particular guest bed in here at least six or eight years ago and I'd always flinched at the first climbing down on the first night home of each trip. More so now, however. And it even led me to reflect on Mama as *Mama,* and Daddy as *Daddy.* I'd have a hard time telling any New York friend of mine why, as an adult, I still called them that. It was a Texas thing, certainly. Broader than that—a Southern thing. But I knew it was more. We'd all just stalled here, in the Dickerson family. We were all still acting out parts from an old script. And my goddam feet were dangling as I thought all this.

I dropped to the floor and padded across the needlepoint rug and out the door and I headed for the steps. I'd lost my connection to sleep and I was going to go downstairs for a midnight glass of wine.

When I reached the top of the staircase I saw a light below. I hesitated, weighing the wine versus a middle-of-the-night conversation with Mama, but maybe the light had been left on accidentally, and if not, maybe this conversation was inevitable anyway, so I started to descend, twisting to see the grandfather clock. It was after two. I landed in the hall and looked toward the light. It came from the parlor and I could see Mama's bare legs and her feet in house slippers stretched out on her settee. I moved to the doorway. She was sitting there sideways, her back

to me, her face lifted to Daddy's portrait. I looked up at him.
The clock ticked loudly behind me. Time had moved on, for
Christ's sake. Let's give it a rest. I almost backed out, but be-
fore I could, she turned her face to me.

"Are you all right?" I asked.

"Can you sit down with me for a few minutes?"

She didn't move her legs off the settee and I looked toward
Daddy's chair and then I chose a neutral corner, a nondescript
overstuffed couch, my mother's attachment to which had always puzzled me. I went to it and sat and it was more comfortable than the brass bed.

"I'm sorry I haven't spent more time with you this trip,"
she said.

"It's me. I've been busy cataloging."

"Missy's going to try again with Jeff, I think."

"Oh shit."

"Don't you talk like that," Mama said, though without any
real fight in her voice.

"Is that what you've been busy doing?" I asked.

"I knew you'd take this attitude."

"There are no secrets between us," I said, meaning we always knew what to expect from each other. But I hit some sort
of nerve. Mama grimaced and looked away from me, toward
the fireplace, though she kept her eyes down, in the smudgy
dark of the inner hearth.

"There are some secrets it's just better to keep," she said.

My distaste for the family's problems had kept me from
trying to sort all this out before. Now I could see the pattern
clearly. Mama's silly hinting around about "things" said to Missy;

the nature of Missy's problem; the decades of silent rancor between Mama and Daddy; even Mama sitting in here in the middle of the night, confronting his image, and then not looking him in the face right now. I knew it all instantly.

"You've already told Missy," I said. "It's time to tell me."

Mama looked at me in surprise. How stupid did she think I was? I could even guess the thing itself. Daddy'd fucked around on her.

"Your father . . ." she began solemnly. Now she looked up at him, setting her mouth hard but her eyes filling with tears. "He wasn't perfect, of course. Far from it. He was a man. Like all men. And what are they like, men? They're just like those bulls of his."

This was Mama's pain—it hurt me to see her tears—and she should be able to say it the way she wanted, but I was impatient at her hemming and hawing. "Mama," I said, making my voice as gentle as I could. "Do you want me to say it for you?"

She looked at me. "No. I can say it. He had women. He slept with women. It was something I knew. And he knew I knew. So did I take the two of you and just up and start over, the first time he let his dick out of the barn?"

Mama clapped a hand over her mouth.

I laughed. She didn't.

"It's not funny," she said, and she was working herself up now. "He makes me mad. He makes me say things I don't want to say. And do things I don't want to do. He still does. But did I tear down the family over a thing like that? Or a dozen things like that? No I didn't. I could never do that. We respect family above all else around here. I hung in. For you and for Missy, and for me, too. I've had all the things I want. So do you think I'm going to tell Missy it's okay to kick that cow chip out the door for his first sleazy fling? You can bet your bonnet I'm not. Do you think I did all this with my own life for nothing?"

And that final question hung in the air, trying to offer its own, presumed self-evident answer, for a long while afterwards. Mama fell silent in its presence and let her gaze retreat to the shadows in the fireplace and I sat thinking how, once she'd made the decision to stay and take it, she'd had no choice but to be who she was—all of it, every last goddam phone call to her daughters, every whine and criticism.

Finally, she flipped her chin up at the painting. "All those trips to New York," she said. "That was one of them. I don't know who she was or where, exactly, except I can see her standing right behind the painter. Maybe she even *was* the painter. Then he put that thing over our fireplace and I've had to look at the twinkle in his eye for decades."

I hadn't noticed the twinkle before, but she was right. He was looking at a woman he was sleeping with. And it occurred to me that the sex part wasn't the crucial thing. I'd never even bothered to think this most obvious thing about his relationship with Mama, and now that I'd heard it as the fact it was, it added absolutely nothing to my complex feelings about him. I understood at once the reason for that. The sense of betrayal, the sense of his commitment to someone else—I'd already felt all that about him over Missy. It wasn't a matter of sex. It was a matter of soft and silly talk and of private understandings. It was a tightly closed circle that by some bone-deep right you should be inside, but you weren't. Quite the contrary. That circle existed to hold you out, and there was somebody else in there with him.

"His *paintress*," Mama sneered. She extended her arm toward him and closed her hand around an invisible brush and she flicked her wrist a few times.

"She wasn't the painter," I said.

Mama looked at me and her arm drooped.

"It's signed 'Gaunt.' That's Jonah Gaunt. He was a minor figure for a while in the photorealist movement of the seventies."

She looked back to the painting. "Well, she was *there*."

"Mama, I'm going to sell it. Daddy's gone. It's all over."

"No it's not. It's passed on to Missy."

This was clearly the moment when our big argument was ready to commence. But that would involve trying to convince Mama she'd made a profoundly wrongheaded decision and wasted her life as a result. She'd never be able to face that, and I honestly didn't want her to. And Missy had to learn this thing for herself anyway.

So I kept my mouth shut.

And we sat for a time in silence in the parlor, my mother and I. Then, without another glance at the image of the man who, both unworthy and dead though he was, still held a perverse power over three grown women, I said good night and went to bed.

*A*t least three grown women.

But I would not go there.

And so, with the lot-sorting done and the estimates fixed and the movers hired and the hotel space booked and the ads placed in the papers, I finished my pre-auction work in Houston, and Mama hadn't criticized me and I hadn't criticized her for the rest of the time I was there, and I never did find the saddle and I never did find anything of Daddy's that made me think to want to keep it, and Friday morning I was back in my office.

Alain was out of the country again and I had final preparations to do for the music auction anyway and it was still a sweet thing to defer my touching this man. I wanted the clutter of Houston and Daddy and all his things out of my head by then. And as I headed for my office and I passed the receptionist with a push-up bra, and then the gangly, weathered-from-being-out-all-weekend-in-a-boat-off-Hyannis beauty of our art director, and then Lydia and her sad eyes, one of the bits of clutter was the thought that there were *other* women in the world—maybe many others—who were shaped and shaken and fucked up by Daddy. Women that Mama and Missy and I would never know about.

I sat at my desk and the thing on top was a letter to our billing office, forwarded to me with a Post-it note from Arthur saying *she must still have a hold on him.* The letter was from Trevor asking for a final statement of account for our "appraisal and any other miscellaneous services." He'd decided *not* to auction off the effects of his recently deceased mother. I shuddered from an unwanted vision of this man, who screwed me in an elevator, crossing that sachet-besotted room, pulling back the comforter—the dozen pillows scattering—and then him crawling in and disappearing there. I backpedaled away from all this.

And I was moved right now to do something I'd been putting off. I picked up the phone and I dialed Missy. The phone rang eight times. Nine. Her answering machine was off. She was gone. I felt a scrabble of panic. Then she answered, her voice thick with sleep.

"Yes?" she said.

"Missy," I said.

"Where are you?"

"I'm back from Houston. I'm in my office."

"Amy," she said, though there didn't seem to be anything intended to follow.

I waited a few moments and then I said, "Missy, are you all right?"

"I was sleeping."

"I'm sorry."

"I need to get up. I just lay down for a few minutes after getting the girls off to school."

"Mama said you're going to try again with Jeff."

"Listen," she said, as if she'd not heard. "Can you come out tomorrow?"

"Missy, what's going on? Is he back?"

"Back? Not yet. No."

"Not yet. So you're expecting him?"

"Look, I need your help. My friend's gone till tomorrow and I need you. She'll pick them up from you after dinner."

"You want me to watch the girls tomorrow?"

"Please."

"While you do what?"

"It's my life, Amy. Isn't it?"

"Yes. Which means it's not Mama's."

"Or yours either. Right?"

"Right." I meant this. Of course I meant this. I needed to stop giving a shit about how this thing came out. If she wanted to turn into Mama, it was her choice.

"I need to see him," she said. "He wants to spend a weekend with me. We're going out to Montauk, as far as we can go out there, you know? Him and me out with the rocks and the seagulls and the potatoes. I need to try to save this."

After a day of Molly clinging and chattering and Maggie standing off and glowering, I got the girls to take a walk in the last hour of light. We bought ice-cream cones on Sea Cliff Avenue and looked at a first edition of *The Tin Woodman of Oz* at the antiquarian book store. Molly had Barbie and Ken in tow and she drifted to a stool to explain books to them while Maggie and I looked at the dust jacket wrapped in Mylar. Dorothy was being held aloft on the joined arms of the woodman and his twin brother.

Both girls knew something nasty was going on in the family, Missy had informed me before she'd driven off to meet Jeff in some unspecified place. Molly just thought there was a big argument, different only in being quite a bit more intense than usual, and that her daddy had gone off on a business trip right afterwards. But Missy was afraid Maggie knew way too much. I'd not had Maggie alone yet.

We bent over the book on the counter, and though the bookman was nearby, Maggie and I had our first moment available for a few private words. And Maggie said, "You know in the movie, there's a guy hanging himself to death in the back of one scene."

"What?"

"You can see it," Maggie said. "It's when they're in the Tin Woodman's forest. Dorothy and the Woodman and the Scarecrow go marching off singing "We're Off to See the Wizard" and right then you can see him doing it in the trees. They even look straight at him as he's dangling and kicking his legs. They just keep on singing."

Before I had a chance to say anything in response—not that I had the slightest idea what that might be—the bookman said, "I'd heard that too."

Maggie looked up at him and then at me. "See?"

I was relieved that this wasn't strictly a personal observation on Maggie's part.

The bookman drew near and put his hand on the counter near the book. He said, "But that's not what's really happening."

Maggie cocked her head at him.

"You can see it better on the big screen," he said. "In fact, it's a stork flapping its wings."

"No it's not," Maggie said.

"The hanging man's an urban legend. It came out of people seeing the movie on TV screens." It was clear from the tone of his voice that he did not own a TV and never would.

"You're *wrong*," Maggie snapped.

The bookman flinched at her vehemence. So did I.

Maggie looked up at me. "It's real," she said. "He just couldn't take it anymore."

The bookman picked up *The Tin Woodman of Oz* and turned his back on us to put it away.

T hen the three of us were at the edge of the cliff. Molly took Barbie and Ken off to the next bench along and she sat them down and pointed out the Sea Cliff harbor and the Sound and so forth to them. Maggie sat close to me on the bench where her mother and I had spoken on my last visit. Maggie was quiet. Molly's voice murmured nearby in the twilight breeze. I waited for a time and then I said to Maggie, low, "Are you doing all right?"

"Duh," she said, meaning, I suppose, that it was a stupid question, of course she wasn't doing all right.

"Do you want to talk about it?"

"About what?"

"Whatever you're not doing all right about."

"Ken and Barbie. Please," she said.

I laughed, too loud. Molly looked our way. I didn't want to draw her to us, so I suppressed the sound instantly. Maggie was right. Molly's dolls were fine, but for her to get into Barbie and Ken was pretty disturbing.

"Now there's a couple that *should* break up," Maggie said.

So the other thing was what was really on her mind.

"Oh I don't know," I said. "They kind of deserve each other, don't you think?"

Maggie laughed, low, secretly, just between the two of us. "I'm never going to get married," she said.

I nodded and made a little sound in my throat to say I understood and I looked away to the harbor. I didn't know, quite, what to understand—much less feel—about this declaration from my ten-year-old niece. She was in pain, or she was just ambitious for herself. She was a smart little modern female, or she was just a child. She hated her daddy, or maybe her mama, or maybe both. She admired her aunt, or she didn't much like what her aunt was but it was all she could hope for, for herself,

"I've already got breasts, you know," she said.

Again, all I could offer was a wee grunt of assent. I glanced at her and her breasts weren't terribly apparent.

"It's from eating too much chicken," she said. "They put hormones in them."

"Oh my god," I said, in facetious shock, trying to change the mood between us. "It's your mama's chicken pot pie."

"Right. Every other night, it feels like."

But then I asked, "Are you angry at her?"

"Because of the chicken?" Maggie said.

"No. That's not it."

"I should be mad at Daddy, don't you think? Doesn't he have a girlfriend somewhere?"

I didn't want to be the one to confirm this. "Is that what you've figured out?" I said.

"It didn't take any heavy figuring," she said. "They didn't mind much who heard them, when they started to fight."

"They're trying to make up this weekend."

"I don't care," Maggie said, and her voice sounded very weary.

I didn't know how to comfort her.

Then she looked me squarely in the face. "You're happy, aren't you?"

"Me?"

"About not having to deal with men?"

"I deal with them."

"But in your job. You make them eat out of your hand. You tell them what's valuable and then you make them pay and you earn a lot of money for it. You like your life."

This last was a declaration. She'd already decided what her aunt was all about and it must have seemed a way out of whatever fix she was in at the age of ten. She was wrong. Very wrong, but she didn't need to hear that right now.

I was aware of a change in Molly's sounds. She was humming and dah-de-dahing a disco beat. I looked and Barbie and Ken were dancing on the bench, Molly kneeling before them, entranced, seemingly happy.

I looked back to Maggie and she was staring intently out at the water. She was not waiting for any answers from me. She had things figured out.

The auctioneer always tries to find one item in a sale that stands out, an item to become emblematic of the excitement and worth of the whole event. Generally this is known as the Pearl of Great Price, an uncharacteristically sappy—not to mention trite—label for our business to use, really, and so

I prefer my personal adjustment of the term—the Pearl of Great *Estimate.* Or, more concisely, the Poge. For example, the Music Manuscript and Vintage Instruments auction that was coming up early the next week was offering a recently discovered, previously unknown holograph manuscript of a chamber piece by Maurice Ravel that he'd titled "Aubade for Violin and Saxophone." This was our Poge, and we were riding it hard, even making a great show of arranging the first known public performance of the piece at the auction. We'd even made it to the front page of the *Times,* though below the fold.

And the sale of the Poge, whatever it is, is always deferred. This is another principle of our business. You make them wait, playing the suspense of it, the delicious anticipation.

All of this was kicking around in my head as I rode the train from Sea Cliff back to the city on that Saturday night. Which was a way of explaining to myself why I was being as patient as I was about Alain. I was content to wait, to deliciously anticipate, to wonder with pleasure, when he'd finally put his hands on me and I'd put mine on him. In the catalog of lots that were my life at forty, I had a strong feeling that he was the Poge, and this is what you did with Poges.

Though it's also true—in the world of the auction—that you never let the Poge go to the *very* end. Those who'd marshaled their resources primarily to buy the Poge would likely refrain from buying anything else until it came up, and then all the losers would walk away empty-handed. You make them wait for a tantalizing while, but then you let them lose early enough so that out of disappointment they'd bid avidly for subsequent lesser items.

Not that I had the slightest idea on the train what the rel-
evance of *that* might be with regards to me and men. Obviously
I'd *already* bid too avidly for much inferior lots. Trevor and Max
and Fred, to name three, and there were others. But of course,
life hadn't produced a four-color slick catalog in advance. Who
knew what was left, out there, that might come your way?

Which might very well be how Jeff was looking at his situation, I thought. Certainly it was how Missy *should* look at hers.

I dipped into my purse and took out my cell phone and I
called my apartment, and I knew why.

I wanted Alain to have called me and the message to be
waiting even then on my machine. By rights, there should have
been nothing. Maybe a resumption of whining and bitching by
my mother. Arthur being his sweetly solicitous self. But Alain's
voice, grainy, crackling, filled my head and I turned to the window, away from the rest of the train car, as if he and I were about
to speak intimately.

"You should be home by now, I believe," he said. "I am so
very sorry to be running around the world again. I have been
missing you. I will certainly be back for the auction this week.
And then we will fly to Paris. Perhaps together, yes? Sweet
dreams, Amy Dickerson."

In front of the dais, the violinist and the saxophonist were
softly tuning up and our Blue Salon was overflowing and I
stood in the shadows to the side, watching the crowd, sort-
ing the faces—there were, of course, many new ones for this
event—and I should have been feeling the rush of an actor's ex-

hilaration—I'd felt it before, just like this, in one of my other lives, waiting for my cue in some play or other—and I'd felt it often in this very room, as I waited to take center stage—*live at the improv, The Female Auctioneer*—and tonight was especially big, with the floodlights of the TV-news operations and the NPR sound engineer on the other side of the dais, ready to record the Ravel premiere for "Performance Today," and I was indeed keyed up, from my starring role, yes—tonight even with an overture—but not as much from that as from the absence of Alain. Here I was again in the midst of this thing I do so well and my mind was preoccupied with a man. A far far better man than the last time, of course, but I wished he was just here and that was that so I could concentrate on what I came here to do and to be. Arthur said Alain was due back soon—his plane had been scheduled in at JFK this afternoon—but it was time to begin and I was picking through the faces once more and there was no sign of him.

Then there was a touch on my elbow. I turned brightly, but it was John Paul Gibbons. I was surprised to see him, though he certainly had more eclectic tastes than most of our clients. "Are you ready to shine for us?" he purred.

"You're the star, John Paul," I said, forcing myself to banter, though I was still feeling distracted. "You and your fine collector's eye."

"And my slut of a checkbook."

"That, too, God bless her," I said.

John Paul laughed. He touched my elbow again. I glanced at his hand there, but averted my eyes at once. I frankly didn't want to look too closely at John Paul Gibbons's hands. He said, "You know, you've promised for ages to have dinner with me."

In fact, I'd deflected his half dozen or so requests for dinner with studied vagueness. "You had your chance in East Hampton a while ago," I said.

"Ah," he said. "Yes."

"Your slut must have gotten jealous," I said. "She clamped her legs shut pretty quick."

"I've regretted it ever since," he said.

"The book bid would have surprised you," I said.

This intrigued John Paul and I knew he was about to ask who the buyer had been, but I'd had quite enough and I said, "Go to your seat now, John Paul. We're about to start."

He gave my elbow another little squeeze and he slid off.

I puffed faintly in exasperation.

I shifted a bit to try to catch the faces toward the back of the room. If Alain was there, he would be standing, but I didn't see him.

Arthur was tapping the microphone with his fingertip. The mike was on and he began his welcome. I tuned it out. I tried to put Alain out of my mind. I was holding my bid-book and I checked, for the third or fourth time, the order bids.

Then Arthur stopped speaking, the crowd applauded and fell silent, and I looked to the musicians. The saxophonist was a youngish man in a tuxedo, prematurely bald with his circling ring of hair lapping down to his shoulders. He licked his reed and looked to the youngish woman who lifted her violin to her chin, cocked her head to meet it, and then nodded, violin and all, at the young man.

The music began very softly, like waking slowly from a deep sleep, and Alain's voice came into my head even more softly. "It is a lover's song of parting," he said. He was suddenly beside me, and from the surge in my chest—part surprise, part relief, part downright scrabbly lust—I moved slightly, though without looking at him, and his lips touched my ear and they lingered there briefly, the words ceasing—it had become a kiss—and the saxophone sighed its shaggy-voiced sigh. "At daybreak," Alain whispered. "Aubade."

I turned my face to him now and he was still very close, smelling not of cologne but of the sun and the sea. "Hello," he mouthed, and I shaped my mouth to the same word, and the music went on, the violin and the saxophone speaking to each other, and even to my untrained ear—I knew little, formally, of music, though I'd studied hard for this auction—to my ear, the music sounded very formal, given what an aubade was, and given what a saxophone was. This was an instrument that had been branded obscene at the turn of the century, too guttural and low-class-sensual for a refined sensibility. And here was Ravel, the neoclassicist, making it refined even in its regret that daybreak had come. Then the two voices fell together more avidly—allegro—and Alain and I were still looking at each other and the violin went silent and the saxophone rasped on and the feeling of it got a little out of hand and then there was serious ardor, the lovers touching, and sure enough the violin rushed back in and Alain's face moved sharply toward the music and he smiled—a lopsided, faintly surprised smile—and I looked to the violin and the saxophone, too, and the sounds were looping and twining and they were not classical at all, they were guttural and low-class-sensual. I turned my face slightly to Alain and he knew at once what I wanted and he bent forward and put his ear next to my mouth and I whispered, "They're not parting. They're making love."

He lifted his face and looked at me and he smiled. "So they are," he said, touching his lips to my ear again. "I did not know Maurice had it in him."

And then I realized why this piece had not come to light before.

When the music had ended, Alain took my hand in his and gave it a brief, gentle squeeze, and then I was on stage and the lights were bright and everyone was focused on me. And I began, still conscious of the place where his hand had touched mine, as if he and I had just had sex in a public place and no one had caught us, no one knew, and I thought how fine a collection I'd made for myself—this collection of hands.

And I was good that night, very good. I sold a Cyrill Demian Flutina, the early-nineteenth-century ancestor of the accordion; a piccolo harp; a dozen letters of encouragement from Toscanini to an aspiring, though ultimately undistinguished, conductor; a working manuscript of John Cage, which I first portrayed, to the delight of a crowd turned out for an impressionist, as ten blank pages, co-opting any negative feelings about him and then going on to build the case for his profound influence on twentieth-century music. I sold the hell out of all of them—and fifty-some-odd other lots, as well—with the Cage manuscript going for six times the estimate. And then it was time for the "Aubade for Violin and Saxophone."

I looked around the room, and bid paddles quivered. There were representatives from major music libraries, universities, and a couple of museums, and my book before me on the podium had bids that already quadrupled the consciously low estimate of twenty thousand that we'd put on the manuscript. I was going to have fun. But first—planning anyway to play a silence while a Brazilian-rosewood harmonium was being toted off—I made a point of finding Alain in the crowd. He was sitting next to Arthur off to my right and I fixed on him and gave him a tiny nod, which he returned.

I began. "The next lot is not simply a previously unknown piece of music by Maurice Ravel, it is a previously unknown Maurice Ravel. He is linked with Claude Debussy as the two titans of musical impressionism, but to a careful ear the two men are so very different. And I mean the two *men*. Debussy was the sensualist. Ravel was the traditionalist, the man of the mind. Until tonight. This piece of music in Ravel's own hand, a thing which someone in this room will soon own, is an image of the secret Ravel. The saxophone that he made speak here was the voice of a sensual man, a passionate man." I looked at Alain. "Who knew Maurice had it in him?"

The crowd laughed. The bidding began. And we ran and ran to a hundred and eighty-seven thousand dollars, and I gaveled it down. It was a very good price for a thing that had no clear market equivalents to affix its value. The crowd knew it was a good price, with a wave of admiring oohs rippling through as testament to that. But at that moment I could only think how weirdly relative the values of things were. I felt the shadow of the tritely corpulent bather in the tiny, third-rate Renoir and the shadow of the man I'd showed off for that night. It had sold for seventy-three thousand dollars more than this thing that seemed to me much more precious.

I looked to Alain, and he brought his hands up in silent applause for me. Arthur noticed the gesture and joined him. How much had I paid for the other men in my life? How much would I pay for my Frenchman with the sharp mind, the good suit, and the ex-dockworker hands?

But there was more to sell. There was some movement around the back fringe of the crowd, and I said, "The real collectors are all sitting still right now." There was a little ripple of self-appreciative laughter at this from the chairs and some of the movement stopped at the edges. "I'm not trying to shame those of you who are slipping out. It's a disappointment to lose the Ravel manuscript, but you can still redeem the evening. Here's lot fifty-nine, for instance." I looked to the turntable and one of the Nichols and Gray young men was just pulling back. There, in the spotlight, lay a lute.

One of the things I love most about my job is the research. Though I richly enjoyed listening to a wide range of music, I was not the least bit musically inclined, and until the week or two before the music auction I knew little or nothing about many objects revered by musicians and collectors of musical things. This lute, for instance, would have seemed odd and pudgy to me. As I considered it on that night, it still did, I suppose, on a gut level, with its bulging, pear-shaped body and stubby neck with the pegbox bent back at a ninety-degree angle. But now, I turned to my room full of acquirers and said, with sincerity, "What a beautiful thing this is, an important example of the resurrection of a venerable sound in the history of music. There may be only two dozen reasonably whole Renaissance lutes still extant. And those have been altered, damaged, or they're of atypical size. *This* lute is one of the very first of Michael Lowe's reconstructions, from 1975, based on Friedman Hellwig's research and the use of X rays to examine existing examples. Made of heartwood yew with maple strips and ebony in the soundboard—and, of course, a beautifully rendered, perforated-rose sound hole sitting at its center—this is a thrilling meditation on the late-sixteenth-century work of Vendelio Venere. Who'll begin at one thousand dollars?"

The estimate was twenty-eight hundred dollars and there were no book bids and I had to hope for a couple of actual lutenists out there, perhaps with an oddball feel for modern history. They seemed to be there: two paddles went up almost simultaneously, from two bidders previously unknown to me, a shaggy-haired young man and a severely bunned middle-aged woman. I let Mr. Shaggy have the benefit of the near tie. "One thousand to you, sir," I said, and then I looked in Ms. Bun's direction and said, "Who'll make it eleven hundred?" And she did.

I played the two up to twenty-one hundred and Shaggy faded and another woman near the front on the left came in and we went exactly to the estimate—two thousand eight hundred dollars—and the new woman dropped out and I thought we were going to come to a close. "Can I have twenty-nine? Twenty-nine hundred? The bass strings on this beauty are red, like the original, but Signor Venere used mercuric sulphide to achieve that effect and slowly, unwittingly, poisoned his customers. Mr. Lowe, I've been assured, has used lead oxide, first cousin to rust, and you can play this lute for decades in safety."

The crowd laughed. "Surely we have more than three lutenists out there. Michael Lowe is already universally understood to be one of only two or three fathers in the rebirth of the lute."

A paddle went up from a jowly, gray-haired man down near the front. "Twenty-nine hundred," I said. "Three thousand?"

Ms. Bun hesitated only a moment and she lifted her paddle. "Three thousand," I said.

These two dueled up to thirty-five hundred and Ms. Bun dropped out and my instincts told me it was over. "Thirty-six?"

No one moved.

"Three thousand six hundred dollars?"

Nothing.

I gave the lute a last look. "And all the music comes out through that exquisite rose," I said, speaking of the sound hole, and my voice was full of tenderness. This seemed—and it was—more an observation for myself than another bit of sales patter. The crowd was still. "Fair warning," I said, and instantly I saw a flickering off to my extreme right. I turned.

For a moment I didn't comprehend what had happened. There was Arthur. Next to him, Alain was gone, a bidding paddle floating in his place. Then I realized that he himself had registered to bid and he was suddenly after this lute. The paddle came down and Alain was looking faux-somber. I set aside my surprise and said, "Three thousand six hundred dollars to the gentleman on my right."

I looked out at the others. I could not imagine Alain playing the lute, not with those hands, though a lute's strings are meant to be plucked, not strummed like a guitar. I suppose a question should have arisen in my mind about whether to gavel this lot down quick, now that my future boss and future lover wanted it. But no such question arose. I said, "Until Michael Lowe made the object you see here, the true and original sound of music by Dowland and Vivaldi and Bach had been lost to the ages. Then it was found once again. History is being made all around us, every day, ladies and gentlemen. Who'll bid thirty-seven hundred dollars?"

I looked at my last bidder, the jowly man down front. I'd noticed, in his earlier run of bids, slim hands, long fingers. He was a musician. I said, "At the preview, some of you may have heard this instrument plucked. She sang beautifully, I'm told. She's among the oldest of the playable lutes in this world and her tones are only now coming into maturity."

Jowly raised his paddle. "Thirty-seven," I said.

In the brief moment it took me to turn back to Alain, his paddle was already up. "Thirty-eight," I said.

And the two men rushed up to forty-four hundred before Jowly stopped. I'd sensed his hesitation instantly and I raised my focus to the others. To rearrange and refresh the bidders' thinking, I occasionally tuck away a bit of Shakespeare, twisting his words to my own purposes, and so now I said, "Gloucester sneers at Richard the Third, 'He capers nimbly in a lady's chamber to the lascivious pleasing of a lute.'" I'd thrown it out there without planning how to make it persuasive, but improvisation exhilarated me when I was at this podium. I looked at the object and I was focused on it and open to the flow of words that always seemed to come to me when I needed it—in short, I was in what the athletes call *the zone*—and I said, "You're bidding for a sweet icon of womanhood—see the rose in her center, and see her belly swollen with your love child."

This selling point surprised even me. The crowd laughed, especially, I think, my regulars, and it was no coincidence that I now noticed John Paul Gibbons about halfway back on my left. He'd suddenly sat up straight.

"She's worth forty-five hundred," I said.

Not that there was any sensible reason for people to bid their money for an object as a result of what I'd just said, but two paddles went up, John Paul's included.

I glanced at Alain and he angled his head to the side with a little smile.

I pointed to John Paul. He was currying favor. And this was just pocket change for him. "Four thousand five hundred dollars to a regular."

Alain flashed his paddle. "Forty-six hundred," I said.

John Paul flashed.

Alain flashed.

John Paul flashed.

Alain seemed to hesitate. I looked at him. He was smiling a faint, aren't-we-having-covert-fun-together smile. "It's against you, Monsieur Bouchard. Will you bid five thousand?"

He gave me a faint nod and lifted his paddle.

I turned back to Monsieur Gibbons. He seemed to be hesitating, as well. He'd come to his senses. I said, "John Paul, I bet you've got your high school guitar tucked away in a special place to play for a special lady. But I'll tell you a secret I bet no woman has yet told you. You need gently to pluck, not strum. The lute, John Paul. The lute's the thing."

My regulars were laughing again, though with a surprised edge—Amy Dickerson has gone *this* far, at last—and the newcomers were beginning to figure out that laughter was okay and they joined in. I wished John Paul was closer because I could swear he was blushing. He kept his paddle down. He had no choice but to drop out. I'd overplayed my hand. But I didn't care. "Fifty-one hundred? No, John Paul? You'll stay with strumming? Anyone? Fair warning." I scanned the room once and then hammered down the gavel. "Sold," I said. "To Monsieur Bouchard for five thousand dollars."

I gave him a last look.

He pursed his lips ever so slightly as if he were kissing my ear.

A fter the last item of the music auction had been sold and the crowd had applauded briefly, and the slow, shuffling exodus had begun, I moved across the dais to my right and Arthur came up and Alain lingered below.

"Lovely, my dear," Arthur said. "You were in top form." He leaned close and lowered his voice conspiratorially. "You certainly squeezed our new boss for every last penny. I think he quite liked it."

"*I* quite liked it," I said.

Arthur giggled and lifted his eyebrows at me in faux shock. He said, "The man's smitten with you, you know."

"I know."

"It can only help." Then Arthur gave me our ritual post-auction congratulatory hug and he let me go and he slid off to the front of the dais where someone was motioning to him. I moved to the steps and paused before Alain, who waited below me. He lifted his hand to help me down. I took it and descended and we stood before each other, a little too close if we wanted to keep our feelings private in this public place, and we shared a nifty little I-want-to-grab-you-and-chew-on-your-face-but-dare-not gaze.

"I have a thing or two to arrange," Alain said.

"About your lute," I said.

He smiled. "About my lute. After that, would you like to dine with me?"

"Of course."

And so he came to lift his glass of wine, letting it float out over the center of the table in the Yalta Restaurant in the East Village, and I lifted mine and moved it out to meet his, and we were about to drink a Bulgarian wine made from misket grapes, a thing Alain had never tried but that the waiter said was good in spite of its modest price, and he'd said yes to it without even a glance at me, a thing that pleased me, oddly, that he was ready to buy a cheap wine on a whim, for its taste, not having to impress me with his money, and he did turn to me as soon as the waiter was gone and say, "It's all right? It sounded like fun," and I liked him even more, and I nodded, so now we touched our glasses and Alain toasted, "To plucking."

I said, "I'm glad you were paying attention."

We drank, and together we studied, with serious faces, the taste of this Bulgarian misket blanc that was called "Blonde," and it was sweetly fruity. "There's a hint of apricot," Alain said.

"Yes," I said. "And the hint of an immature democracy."

"I see what you mean," he said. "Should we send it back?"

"No. I'm enjoying the ideological struggle of it." I took another sip.

He laughed, softly, as a kind of afterthought. "It was a great pleasure to watch you manipulate our clients tonight," he said.

I liked his "our." It felt as if he'd drawn a circle around the two of us.

I said, "I wanted more for the Ravel manuscript. It seemed such an important thing."

"You got more than I expected."

"Thanks for giving me an angle on it, the things you said about the secret Maurice."

Alain shrugged. "I was sincerely surprised by the work. The few other times he'd used a saxophone, they were strictly governed by his classical sensibility. In the 'Bolero' he uses them."

"I despise that piece," I said.

His eyes widened.

"I'm sorry," I said. "It's one of your favorites."

"No. On the contrary. I despise it, too. My look was one of surprise. Our shared opinion is quite rare for laymen."

"I have to tell you, personally, I'm relieved," I said, and I was. "Any man who thinks 'Bolero' is great lovemaking music must surely be a bad lover. It's one long male delusion about passion. Pump pump pump, slow fast faster, soft hard harder. It's all linear and repetitive. Now I'm willing to bet you don't make love like that, Alain."

Alain sat back in his chair. He seemed a little breathless, though perhaps I was projecting. *I* was breathless, certainly. "No I do not," he said.

We fell silent for a time, sipping at our Bulgarian wine.

"She's not so bad, this blonde," Alain said, pouring more for both of us.

I took up the glass and said, "I've been meaning to ask."

"Yes?"

"Why that lute?"

"Ah," he said, smiling what felt like a private smile.

"Do you play?" I asked.

"No, not at all," he said. "I am intrigued by the lute as . . . how shall I say it? As an icon, perhaps. It is very feminine, as you pointed out. You know, in Flemish, the word for lute, *luit,* was also the word for a woman's most tender sexual part. And in Venice, the courtesans carried the lute as a badge of their trade. Some of them were independently famous for their skill as players. And in my own country, there was a lovely woman poet, Louise Labé of Lyon, who wrote quite openly in the sixteenth century about desire and the power of sex, and one of her poems was to her lute. 'Lut, compagnon de ma calamité, De mes soupirs témoin irreprochable, De mes ennuis controlleur véritable, Tu as souvent avec moy lamenté.' Do you understand?"

"A little."

"She says to her lute that it is her companion in adversity— over a departed lover, clearly—and the lute laments with her and moderates her troubles. She goes on to say that even when she begins to play some delightful air, her lute changes her tone to a lament, as if the lute itself has sensed her deeper need and makes her . . . as she says, 'En mes ennuis me plaire suis contreinte, Et d'un dous mal douce fin espérer.' That is to say, she is forced—by her lute—to find her pleasure in grief and hope for sweet endings to so sweet a pain."

He fell silent and I found my hand with its own desire at this moment. I reached across the table and laid my palm on his right temple. I wanted to kiss his mind. He reached up and took my hand and kissed me in the palm. He let my hand go and it came back to me, reluctantly. I was having just a bit of trouble breathing and I suppose that scared me a little, the letting go of a certain kind of control, and so I said, "If I'd known all that, I would have been able to make you pay even more."

He smiled—at my cheekiness, I think. I usually valued that trait in myself, as well, but I was suddenly appalled by it. I'd broken this mood of his, I was afraid, a mood I felt was uniquely part of him—all at once intellectual and romantic and faintly pretentious, too, though not offensively so, more boyishly so, or up-from-the-docks-of-Marseilles-and-still-delighted-by-what-it-turns-out-I-can-do so—I truly liked this man and I had to accept being breathless, now and then, with him.

He said, "I would have paid whatever it took."

"Yes."

"I bought a painting recently," he said. "From a museum in Budapest. I had friends there and they knew I had loved it for years. So when they were refocusing their collection, they let me purchase it. It was painted by Parrasio Micheli, a Venetian artist, done about the time Louise Labé wrote her sonnet. It is an image of Venus playing a lute. The lute is almost exactly the lute I bought today. Her garment has fallen off her shoulders and her breasts are bare and she is playing the lute and Cupid is beside her, leaning on her thigh, staring at the rose in the lute's center. He stares quite lovingly and with a little bit of guilt, as if it is his goddess's *luit* he is looking at. Do you understand?"

"I do."

"She holds the lute just so, beneath her lovely, naked breasts, and her face is lifted. She is singing, and I stare at her now on the wall of my apartment in Paris and I strain to hear the song that she sings."

I do not play a musical instrument. I do not sing. These things filled me with regret as I listened to Alain across the table that night. He fell silent, sipping his cheap Eastern European wine and thinking about Venus on his wall. Then he looked at me, abruptly, as if waking from a dream, and he said, "I look forward to showing you Paris."

"Soon, yes?"

The waiter was suddenly beside us with pelmeni and caviar and we turned our attention to the food. And when we returned to words, we spoke of minor things through the rest of the dinner—the fineness of the beluga, the chill of the borscht, the tenderness of the lamb in Alain's Azu, the way the bidding went that evening for the Ravel manuscript and the harmonium and the Toscanini letters, the weather in New York and the weather in Paris, the relief we were feeling at switching to a very nice 1985 Coppola Rubicon.

But at the same time my mind was following little daisy chains of associations: Venus would come to me and link to Alain standing before her in his apartment and that image would

link to Alain's own newly acquired lute and then to the plucking of its strings and to his hands and to my little fantasy of him
loading and unloading ships on the docks in Marseilles, and
then, over fruit crêpes, I let the next link in that particular chain
find voice. I said, "I keep thinking you must once have worked
with your hands."

He furrowed his brow and tilted his head slightly. "Such as?"

A tiny-toothed panic began nibbling in my head—Alain's
face could simply be registering puzzlement, but I was afraid
he was somehow offended. Still, I plunged ahead. "Oh, like, a
stevedore or something."

"No, nothing like that at all," he said and though he was
not smiling at the suggestion, his forehead had smoothed out
and he seemed okay.

"I didn't mean to . . ."

One of the hands that started this all came out to the center of the table to reassure me. "It's all right. I am just curious
what made you think this."

I nodded at the hand.

He looked but did not comprehend.

"Your hands seem very powerful. Like they grew up working at something quite physical," I said, and then I added,
emphatically, "I *love* your hands." I said this to prevent a further furrowing of his brow, to make sure there would be no
misunderstanding. But this open and direct declaration of regard for a part of his body sucked the air out of me.

"Thank you," he said. "But it is strictly genetic, I'm afraid."

I put my hand on top of his. "However they came to be
like this is fine with me."

We looked at each other for a long moment, and he said, "You were wonderful tonight at the auction. You were everything Arthur said you were, and more."

"It's strictly genetic," I said.

"However you came to be like this is fine with me," he said, and we kept straight faces for each other. Then he said, "You don't mind if I speak a tiny bit of business?"

"I don't mind."

"The deal is completed now."

"To buy Nichols and Gray?"

"Yes. It is what you call a done deal."

"Shall we drink to that?" I said.

"Yes," he said. "Let's."

Alain poured out the rest of the Rubicon and we touched glasses.

"To Bouchard, Nichols and Gray," I said.

"Bouchard will be a very distant partner to the business," he said. "To Nichols and Gray."

We touched glasses and drank. There was a hint of something like chocolate in it this time that I hadn't noticed before. I put down my glass.

"Amy," he said, "have you thought about the offer?"

"For me to stay on?

"Yes."

"Of course."

"Do you think you will accept it? Tonight I saw who is the soul of this business."

"Don't I get a trip to Paris first?"

"Of course." Alain put his glass down and reached out and

laid his hand on the table, turning his palm up to me. I placed my hand on his, palm to palm. He said, "You know that the auction business will be a very tiny portion of my company. This is good. It's what makes it possible for us to touch like this."

"Yes."

"But it also means that occasionally I will be occupied with other things. My heart wants more than anything to be with you in Paris. Tonight. I would, under other circumstances, say to you, Let's go to the airport this very moment. We will catch a cab in front of the restaurant and go to my city. But instead I have to fly in the morning to the Middle East. I have perhaps two weeks of urgent business having to do with jet planes. So I ask you please to be patient with me. I'll bring you to Paris at the first opportunity. Do you understand?"

"I do." And I did, on a practical level. But I needed something more.

"My feelings for you," he said, "are not casual things. You know not so very much about me. I was never a stevedore, I'm afraid. I grew up quite comfortably as the son of a diplomat— I believed I mentioned my father to you—but more relevantly, my paternal grandfather acquired modest wealth in the company he owned and wished someday to pass on to me. It made machine tools, simply, and I went eventually to your Harvard Business School. My grandfather died and I took his machine tool business and I have made it into much more than that and I have made many times more money than he did, or my father, either, of course. I say these things because it is what I do in the world and it is important for me to tell you who I am apart from my hands which you love. Do you understand?"

I could only nod. Whatever more I'd needed, he was doing a good job of providing.

He said, "I am married and divorced twice. One a French girl, one an Austrian. They are no longer in my life at all. I have no children. If I seem always to be running away from you, it is not because my feelings for you are of no substance."

"I understand, Alain."

"I want Paris to be perfect for us. Can you wait?"

"Yes."

On the sidewalk, with the chauffeur opening the back door of the black-windowed stretch, Alain and I confronted the unspoken question of exactly *how much* we would wait on. We hesitated and gave each other the your-place-or-mine look and came up with no answer. I slid into the backseat ahead of Alain and he said to the driver, "Head uptown and if you get to One-hundredth Street go back down again." Then Alain was in, and the door was closed, and we were invisible to the city, and as the car began to roll, his arms were around me and my two hands were at the back of his head pressing his face into my kiss.

There was no direction, no rush, to our touching. We kissed and kissed and his mouth was soft and it was pouty and floppy-lipped and his tongue tasted lightly tart and dusty with cherry tones and a hint of chocolate and one of his hands was on the small of my back and one had come around me and was on my shoulder, and eventually the hand on my back vanished for a time, and then it was on the front curve of my shoulder, and then it was on my breast, and I moved my own hand through his hair at the back of his head to tell him it was all right, and he knew things—he knew not to rub or to squeeze but to cup and slightly to lift—and my breast rose with his touch and I took my hands away from him and I slid them between us and I began to unbutton my blouse, and our lips parted and kissed and parted again, and he pulled back to watch me and his eyes were bright from the night streets of the city coming through our dark window and his eyes were full of tenderness, I could see, and my blouse was undone, and I shrugged off the cloth, and my breasts were naked before him and nipple-tight, and he took a deep, appreciative breath, and it occurred to me that he was imagining me holding a lute, and I lifted my arms to him and he came to me and kissed my lips one sweet brief moment and then his face fell to my breasts and his lips were on me and he knew to pluck.

And so we made do for a long while with our hands and our lips and my breasts. Then, comfortable in our moist ardor, awash in the neon of storefronts passing outside, we paused and held each other. My hands had refrained from touching him in a more private way, and his hands, too, had been content with my naked breasts, holding back from the secrets of my luit, and now, sighing together, letting our breathing slow, we put our hesitation into words. I said, "This is lovely."

"Yes," he said.

"Which is why I think . . ." I hesitated briefly to find just the right way to say it.

And he took up the thought at once. "We should wait . . ."

"Yes. For Paris."

"For the opportunity to linger."

"Without passage the next morning."

"Passage for one."

"And we wait for Paris," I repeated.

"For Paris," he said. "Thank you, yes, mon amour, for my Paris."

He had just called me his love, I knew, but it was not in the language we primarily shared and so I registered it mostly with my mind, though my mind adored it, and I burrowed deeper against him and he held me more tightly and he touched the intercom button and gave the driver the address of my apartment and we said no more and kissed no more for a long while, we simply held each other, which was just right for now and which was another true thing this man knew about women.

Then we were before my building and my breasts were covered once more and we kissed one last sweet time and he said, "Till Paris" and I said, "Till Paris."

I crossed the sidewalk and passed under the awning, and I'd had a little too much to drink and my head was full of clutter: it's right that we're doing this right and I should turn around now for a last good-bye but I can't see him anyway through the black windows and my lips are tingling and my nipples are too and it's good and I should turn and wave even if he can't see me. But I was through the door and the doorman was circling out from behind his desk, and he had his arms full of roses, and I knew who they were from. I turned and the limousine was gone. I turned back and took the roses into my arms and I could see the card and it said "You are a treasure. Alain."

"A package came for you also," the doorman said—Wayne the doorman, old enough to be my father, with a weathered face, and at that moment, with these roses in my arms, I liked Wayne as I'd never liked him before, and I gave him a very big smile.

"Could you bring it up, Wayne?"

"Of course, Ms. Dickerson. I'll be right behind you."

"You're a dear," I said, and I went to the elevator, wanting to concentrate entirely on Alain's roses, three dozen long-stemmed reds. And this I did, going up in the elevator, and elevators were suddenly redeemed for me. The world had turned and I thought again how this was right.

In my apartment I had to clear the umbrellas out of their stand—a six-gallon Red Wing stoneware butter churn—to have a thing large enough to keep all the roses together. I dropped a couple of aspirin in the water to help the flowers stay fresh—grateful at last for one of my mother's helpful tips to make my home beautiful just in case. And I had sense enough to put the churn in place to the left of my fireplace before putting in the water and the flowers because the arrangement turned out to be massive and heavy. I was on my knees arranging their faces just so, taking in their scent, recollecting the touch of Alain's tongue on mine, and the knock at the door startled me. I'd forgotten about the parcel.

Wayne was full of apologies for the delay, and I stepped aside for him to bring in a rectangular box about yard long. He went away and it sat before my couch and I approached it. I recognized the Nichols and Gray address label. It still did not occur to me what was in it. I took the scissors I'd used to trim the rose stems and I ran it along the tape on the box and I opened the flaps, and there was the lute.

I pulled back, thinking there must be some mistake. I looked at the label. It was, of course, addressed to me. But this was Alain's. I put my hands upon its neck and I drew it from the box and held the curve of its belly against my own. I leaned to the box and peeked in. There was no note. Nothing. Just the lute suddenly in my arms. I could not hold it. I laid it carefully on the couch, propping it into the pillows. Its central rose drew me to it. I extended my hand and ran the tip of my finger over the cut-out swirls. But I still assumed this was a mistake.

I thought to call Alain, to tell him not to worry, someone had mistakenly addressed his lute to me. I moved around the couch and to the phone, and with the night and the roses and now this object having strayed into my possession, I had not noticed the hotly burning 3 on my machine.

I touched the play button. The first was Missy. I hadn't spoken with her since she'd taken off to Montauk with Jeff. She said, "I'm sorry this thanks is late, but thanks for taking care of the girls. You'll be glad to know that the happy marriage has not been restored . . . I'm sorry. I didn't mean it that way. I'm saying you'll think you were right, because Jeff and I still haven't reconciled, but you'll forgive me if I don't just go, Okay, my course is clear . . . Whatever. I just wanted to say thanks."

I should have skipped over Missy here. I didn't want all these further confused feelings from and for my sister on this night. This was *my* goddam night and it had been swell and the only should-I-stay-with-it-or-should-I-not question I wanted to think about was over me and this lute. I deleted her message and the next was Alain and my breath caught at the mere sound of his voice.

"Hello, Amy. I am in Arthur's office and you and I are about to have dinner in a little Russian place I know, and when you hear this message, we will have kissed some and you will have found the lute. Yes. She is yours. She was always intended to be yours. I gave her a long, sweet kiss on the rose and now she is for you."

A single, uninflected tone of bafflement blared in my head now—though maybe it was simply the answering machine's tone signaling the end of the message—and I tried to cut it off. This was a wonderfully sweet and charmingly improvised gesture, a loving thing, a geste d'amour. And now I was hearing Alain's voice again, in message number three. "The door of the automobile is barely shut," he said. "I have lost you from my arms and from my sight, but perhaps you already have your arms full of roses. I am so very sorry we are not together all the night long, but we are right to wait just a little. Good night, Amy."

The answering machine blared and stopped and its fussy man's voice said there were no more messages. I turned and faced the roses, and the couch had its back to me, and just out of sight in the pillows was the lute. I circled to stand before her. I angled my head to match her angle as she lounged there like the Naked Maja. This was how I was trying to sense the object—as *her,* as an icon of womanhood—I could hear Alain ask me the question he asked more than once—*Do you understand?*—and I stood before the lute and worked on that. And I tried to understand why understanding this was not an immediate and happy thing. I did not play the lute. No one, surely, ever assumed I played the lute. And I saw this clearly as an *instrument,* as a thing to be played—it was only twenty-five years old, after all, not exactly an object transcendent with age, no matter what auctioneering spin I'd put on it tonight. So what? So this. I knew what I was thinking of. I was thinking of a goddam useless-to-me horse saddle. A beautiful saddle. And that made me mad. Get the hell out of this, Daddy. This lute was nothing like a saddle. It was *not* just a utilitarian thing, it was an object of beauty, as well. That's how it was offered. It had meaning in that way for Alain. I could understand that meaning. And it actually seemed a sexy and special thing to me—in my *mind,* at least—for a man to elaborate his appreciation for women in this lovely, metaphorical way.

I realized that another part of my discomfort was the thought that the lute had come here to challenge me. I sat beside her. Alain did not intend it, I knew. But was she asking me to do something? *Be* something? Was I to learn to play the lute? No. She was simply an object, a lovely object, and I took the lute up by its throat and stood and I looked around my living room to find a place for it. Nothing came to mind. I could move this lamp, that vase, I could lean it against a wall, I could try to find a way to hang it—perhaps a thin, almost invisible cord around its neck—and *this* shouldn't have been so difficult either, finding a place for this thing. My apartment had plenty of air in it, plenty of available spaces for another object, and I was eclectic in my tastes. This would fit in quite beautifully, really, and I looked at the fireplace.

The roses were on one side. I stepped forward and moved the stand of fireplace implements around to the other side and I leaned the lute there. That was fine. I stepped back. I was missing Alain, I realized. I wanted him here, before this fireplace, on this couch, in my arms. Perhaps I resented the lute for his absence. Not really. It was fine where it was. It was beautiful. And she was a pear-shaped girl, somebody's older sister, wide in the hips. No threat at all. *I* was somebody's older sister. But I was still thin. And Alain Bouchard was clearly smitten. And I was a little bit drunk, I knew. And a little bit bummed out about not being with Alain. About waiting. About Daddy, too. I didn't like him intruding here, which he'd already done. And I didn't like all his stuff hanging over me, unsold. I'd push that along. Arthur had already put our logistics people on the task of setting up the place in Houston for me, running the estate sale ads. Arthur was sweet. I hoped he was with a nice man tonight.

I sat down on the couch and I knew it was time to sleep. I'd start right here, right on this comfy couch, and then move to the bed sometime in the night. I could do this any damn way I wanted because I was alone. I stretched out and looked over to the lute. I blew her a kiss good night.

I wanted to be in Paris. But I had to go to Houston. Ten days and two calls from the Middle East later I was in my father's house once more, a house I was there to wrench from his dead hands at last. The calls were brief and I was glad to get them, too glad by far, I suppose. But why too glad? Alain said,

"Amy I'm calling from Dubai." And, "Amy I'm calling from Cairo." He said, "I miss you very much." And, "I can't wait till I see you." He said, "I must go now." And, "Tell me you are thinking of me." "I'm thinking of you," I said. And, "I touch the places you touched." At this, spoken to him in Egypt, he sighed a sigh I could hear even over the transatlantic static and over a sound in the background like a jet engine.

In Houston there would be no calls. I told him I would go and do this thing in a city that was foreign to me now and he told me it would not be long before he was in the city that was his home and he would phone me when I returned to New York and after that we would be together.

Mama greeted me on the porch when I arrived, and right behind her were Molly and Maggie and then Missy, too. I hadn't expected them. I was glad I'd gone up to the porch without my bag because instantly I lied that I'd booked a hotel room this time and I left them all standing there as if they'd been expecting something from me, though none of us could quite figure out what it was.

I came back that evening. The girls were in bed. Mama and Missy were sitting in the parlor. Daddy's portrait was propped up with a lot-tag on it in a ballroom at a chain hotel near the Galleria, and over the fireplace was its ghost—a vast, clean, eggshell-white rectangle showing us how dingy the walls had grown all around. The pony-skin chair was gone. Everything of his gone. The door to his den was standing open and I could see the empty space, the empty bookshelves. Arthur's local-hire Lifters and Movers had done this drastically symbolic thing while I was far away and unaware.

Mama was on her settee and I sat down on the overstuffed couch at the opposite end from Missy. We sat in silence for a time, as if I'd interrupted something private between them and they had no energy to fake some other conversation.

I couldn't keep my eyes off where Daddy's image had hung.

"So it's all gone," I said.

Mama raised her face to the empty space, as well.

"I still don't think it's right," Missy said in a wee voice and Mama and I simultaneously shot her a hard glance.

She looked at Mama and then at me and she veiled her eyes. She seemed very young. "I miss him," she said. "If you don't, that's your thing. I do. I'm not ready to auction him off."

Nobody said anything for a long while.

Then Mama cocked her head at the empty space. "It's *not* all gone," she said. "Not till it's sold or dumped."

Which wasn't what I expected of her. I figured after that long pause, given time to reflect on her baby's dissolving marriage, on the repudiation of her own choices that a divorce would represent, on her commitment to Texan family values enduring forever, she'd tone all this down a bit for Missy's sake.

Missy rose abruptly and went out of the room.

Mama looked at me. "I don't have the strength for this anymore."

"Good," I said. "I think that's good."

She looked sharply away as if I'd just rebuked her.

"I mean it, Mama. It's time you stopped arguing with him and worrying about us. It's time for yourself."

She fluttered her hand at me to end the conversation.

I got up and followed Missy.

As I entered the staircase hall, the front door clicked shut. I went to the door and hesitated a moment, but then I followed my sister.

She was standing on the porch, surveying the yard.

I stood beside her. Out in the dark, in the direction of our pin oaks, a mockingbird was singing like one bird after another that it wasn't.

"You didn't come down because of the auction, did you?" I asked.

"What do you think? I don't like this."

"She's not trying to take Daddy away from you."

"Who knows what she's trying to do? She'd have me keep Jeff while she's selling Daddy off? Do you really think you understand her?"

I could tell her Mama was having a change of life. I could tell her the way to reconcile Mama's advice was for her to sell off Jeff and Daddy both, that Mama was probably going to come around to that point of view herself eventually. But I said nothing.

The mockingbird did the ricochet call of a cardinal. And again. And then the sweet, watery trill that blue jays sometimes do and it surprises the hell out of you because you think they're just mean squawkers. And the blue jay one more time, a little slower, in a lower pitch. I thought that maybe I shouldn't be hearing the mockingbird's voices as an identity crisis. Maybe he was a collector.

"You know, she told me about Daddy's running around," Missy said.

"You heard it before me."

"I still love him," she said.

"I do too," I said.

We both scowled into the dark for a few moments, not having intended that little declaration. For me, at least, it made things sound too simple. Surely it was too simple for her, too.

I looked at Missy. We each of us had an old steamer trunk stuck away in some corner of our head and inside were all the bits and pieces we kept of him. Him and me moving together in an exhibition hall, sizing up cattle; us standing at attention for the moon landing, his hand on the top of my head; me laying the back of my hand against his leg with us looking out from our fence line. Missy had whatever—some moment on his lap, an aren't-you-beautiful twinkle in his eye, a well-timed kootchy-koo—she had a thousand of those.

Then she said, "I can't believe you're so anxious to sell off all his stuff."

"That's Mama's call."

"You're only too ready to do it."

"She'd let you take anything you want, if you asked her."

"That's not the point."

"If she doesn't want it and you don't really care to have it, what *is* your point?"

"Oh, come on, Amy. You know more than anyone that stuff isn't just stuff. It's him, isn't it? Isn't that what we're doing here? Getting rid of *him*?"

She was right, of course. That's what we were doing and I knew it. I'd just played dumb with her about this—why? To antagonize her. To make her say it for herself. Why was I such a shit to my own sister when I wouldn't be to anyone else?

"I'm sorry," I said.

"For what?"

"I don't know why we're always at each other's throat over something. I'm sorry for that, for my part in that."

She didn't say anything. Not, I'm sorry for my part. Not, I forgive you. She just kept her mouth shut, though she sagged a little bit, leaned against a porch pillar. It was all right. I wasn't expecting anything back, which made me realize I really *was* sorry.

There was a rustle and a faint tracking of wings and then silence. The mockingbird had flown away. I looked into the dark, beyond the yard, down the street a ways, from one lit porch to the next. On the other side and a couple of houses down, I recognized, even in the dark, a curved portico, tapered columns.

I said, "Do you remember the . . . what was their family name? Clayton, I think. The Claytons down there? I sold you to the daughter. Wendy, it was. Wendy Clayton. I held a play auction and she wanted a little sister and I sold you to her."

I looked at Missy. She was still leaning against the pillar but had turned her face to me and had narrowed her eyes.

"You don't remember this," I said.

"No. You sold me?"

"You were three."

"Are you sorry for that, too?"

This wasn't going all that well. I looked back to the street. "Yes," I said. "I'm sorry I sold you."

"I don't remember growing up down there."

"The deal didn't go through."

"Ah," Missy said, like that explained everything.

"I thought I'd told you this before," I said.

"Was it buyer's regret?"

I looked at her.

"That the deal didn't go through," she said.

"No. Wendy was happy enough."

"It wasn't seller's regret." Missy said this matter-of-factly.

"I was seven," I said.

Missy nodded. We fell silent for a while, and her mind clearly tracked far away, because she finally said, "I can't re-invent myself just like that. I bought into the family stuff big time. There's no diversity in my portfolio."

This last was a sneer. I didn't like to think how Jeff might have used that stupid line on her in the last few days.

"I understand," I said.

"No you don't. You don't understand. I've got a B.A. in English and my last job was organizing our Tri-Delt 'Hearts for the Arts' Valentine ball my junior year. What are my options?"

I almost said, Alimony and child support. But I didn't. I understood her point.

"And you know what gets me?" she said. "Mama trying to have it both ways. For me it's, Think of the girls and keep the family together. Fine. For her it's, Auction every last thing off so Mama can go on. Fine. But she can get rid of Daddy because she has all his money."

"And no kids," I said.

"And no kids. We're not kids."

"No."

"But I feel like one," Missy said. "I feel as helpless as the toddler you sold down the river."

"Down the street."

"Maybe you're both right. Maybe I've got to let him go too. He gave you the career. He gave me jack shit."

My first, very superficial, reaction to this was to think, No, Missy, you're wrong, he hated my career. But that didn't last long. She was right. He'd always taken me seriously, Daddy. He'd made me keep up, pay attention. He treated me like a Texas son. He made it possible for me to do what I did.

I turned around to face Missy. In spite of the anger at Daddy, there seemed to be no real fight in her. Her head lolled sideways against the pillar. She was right about me, I thought, but wrong about herself.

I said, "But he gave you all the love."

"Was that what it was?" she said and she didn't lift her head and she didn't look at me and her voice was so faint and seemed so full of something dark that my limbs went suddenly leaden and I had to work to hold myself up.

"Missy," I said and I put my hand on her arm, and my panic and my saying her name and my touching her all went before the first conscious shaping of an image of Missy on his lap—a thing I'd seen a thousand times—and now I wouldn't let myself see his hands.

Missy picked up on my state and turned her face to me and she looked at me closely and knew at once what I was thinking. "No," she said emphatically. "No, I didn't mean that." She squared around and took my two hands in hers. "Are you thinking that Daddy . . . ? God no, Amy. He never did anything wrong like that. I swear."

"Are you sure?"

"Yes. I'm sure." Her eyes held steadily on mine. She was focused and she was calm, in spite of this thing I'd raised. My panic dissolved and I squeezed her hands tightly.

"Okay. I'm sorry," I said.

"Jesus, Amy."

"I'm sorry."

"I just meant . . . he loved me, yes, he made over me a lot, but what did I get from all that? Stunted growth. I never wanted to stop being his little Missy girl."

We realized now that we were still holding hands and we let go.

Missy shuddered. "I can't believe you thought that, even for a moment."

I had no answer. I looked out into the night, thinking how it was true, I was ready to believe that of Daddy. Instantly. And the corollary was that I was ready to believe Missy, instantly, in such a charge against him. She was my sister.

I love my job. I am the maker of crucial connections. Between the passion in a heart for an object outside it and the object itself. Between the self and its defining act of acquiring a certain thing of this world. And in that transaction, my own passion flows both ways—through the object desired and through the one who desires it. I become part of both. I value and I am valued. I collect and I am collected.

But I did not love my job the next day. I was in a hotel ballroom with garish glass chandeliers and soda-cracker-white walls and filled with the ghosts of sales-rep conventions and junior-league banquets. Rows and rows of padded metal-stack chairs were arrayed before me and scattered about on them was a wildly mixed lot of absolute strangers. And all around the vast room were Daddy's things.

And I sold them. Mama was not there and Missy was not there. I was alone, and I told myself I was just an auctioneer, that's all. We had antiques dealers in attendance who knew the value of some things and were interested only in getting them at a fraction of that value, and we had civilians who actually wanted some things, though mostly casually, as long as it was a bargain. But that was okay. It didn't make any difference. Mama had said to me the night before, Honey just do the best you can but I don't really care how much money comes out of all this, just sell it all off, make sure not one bit of it comes back to me.

So I sold his quarter-repeater pocket watch for eight hundred dollars and his naked-breasted pre-Columbian woman for six hundred and his Calvinist King James for four hundred and on and on. These weren't great prices but it was the best I could do. I sold them. A hundred lots. More. I moved them out. All of them. The dealers got their keystones and better. The civilians got their bargains. And then his portrait came up.

The two hotel guys who'd been working the floor carried it forward and leaned it against the lot table to my left, angled slightly toward me, and they stepped away.

It was just Daddy and me, face to face for the last time. I was struck by how large this thing was. And by how it was *him*.

"Lot number one hundred twelve," I said. "Portrait of . . . a Texan. By Jonah Gaunt." I turned to the faces in the chairs.

There were sixty or seventy scattered around. There'd been a great deal of coming and going. I'd long ago stopped trying to read these faces. I just looked for the numbered cards going up. Daddy was staring out at them, too, and maybe Mama was right, he was looking at us all with the twinkle of adultery in his eyes, but I didn't care about that at the moment. The point was, this was Daddy, whatever he was. It was Daddy and he was facing a room full of strangers and I had to make one of them love him.

No. The *image* of him, I reminded myself. It was simply the image of him they had to love. Get a goddam grip, Amy.

The estimate I'd put on him was four thousand dollars. All the estimates had proved to be high. I didn't know where to begin.

I stole a glance in his direction.

And I asked what the passion was in my own heart.

It was to sell.

I confronted this raggedy band of mostly ignorant, tight-fisted buyers and I said, "Who'll start with one thousand dollars?"

No one.

I said, "Some of you surely know the name of Jonah Gaunt, and if you don't, then that's the reason you should bid now. The man will someday take his place with Richard Estes and Chuck Close as one of the important photorealists of the twentieth century. He worked with them. He partied with them. He saw the world the way they saw it. And you can see his expert hand here in this Texan. One thousand?"

Again, nothing.

Suddenly I felt bad for him.

I turned to him. I said, "You can look into his eyes and expect him to speak. And he'll know you. Here's a man who will know your passion for hard work and open spaces and the old-time virtues and the two-step and Lone Star Beer." And I was suddenly popping little flares of him—Daddy on the dark porch drinking a beer and me sitting very still nearby, listening to the night, and he nudged me and offered me a sip and I took it, and it tasted like pee, I said, and he jerked the bottle back; Daddy Texas-two-stepping with Mama at Gilley's—maybe it was Gilley's, maybe somewhere else—but I was watching them dance while keeping an eye on Missy and we were kids, and then she and I finally did a little walk-around ourselves, two-stepping around the table, me being Daddy and Missy being Mama.

And Daddy was pretty hard to face like this, me flashing on a dead past while standing before these passionless strangers, these dilettantes, these garage-sale whalers, and I forced my selling words away from the concrete things—the collectibles—and back to the abstractions. "And he knows your taste for taking risks and getting ahead and being your own man and it's all in this face as real as your own best pal."

And through this all, I was fixed on Daddy's face, I was looking him in the eyes, staring down his twinkle, and I was saying too much, I knew, and it didn't mean anything anyway to these people. I dragged myself away from him and back to the metal-stack chairs and I said, "So who'll start the bidding for a thousand dollars?"

No one.

"Okay," I said. "Maybe we're expecting too much of him."

Maybe we were. Especially now that he was gone.

"Who'll start for a hundred dollars?"

No one.

I understood. I felt the same thing. He was enormous. But he was a stranger.

Then a hand went up in the back row of chairs. I could see only the hand and it had no bidding number.

"All right," I said. "You're without a bid number, but you can get that after the fact. To the person in the back row, a hundred dollars."

And with her hand still raised, Missy peeked around from behind the man in front of her.

I found myself relieved. "Fair warning," I said at once. And then, "Sold. To the woman in the back row for one hundred doilars."

There were half a dozen boxes of books, a couple of shotguns left. I sold them quickly and the buyers scattered just as quickly and I came down from the podium and Missy was still sitting in the back.

I approached her.

"Hey," I said.

"Hey."

I was beside her. She stayed seated and her face was turned up to me.

"I'm really sorry," I said, though I would have had no clear answer if she'd demanded I tell her for what.

But she didn't. She said, "Me too," and lowered her face.

I looked at the top of her head. The white track of her part, the fall of her hair with the tips of her ears poking through—I was filled with a sudden tenderness for my little sister.

I didn't know what to do about it, so I just kept talking.

"What are you going to do with it?" I said.

"It's canvas, isn't it?" she said, keeping her face down.

"Yes."

"I'll roll it. Put it away somewhere."

We fell silent and did not move. My pulse thumped softly in my ears. I closed my eyes and my head was empty and I opened my eyes again.

"I'm leaving Jeff," Missy said.

"Whatever I can do," I said.

"Thanks."

And still she kept her face down, my little sister. So I lifted my hand and laid it gently on the top of her head. Then, after a moment, her own hand came up and touched mine.

A week later I was sleepless on Air France Flight 9. I wedged the pillow against the window, the Atlantic Ocean dark beneath me and the night sky all around, and I closed my eyes and I opened them again. My head was full of jet hum. I wasn't sleeping, but my mind had lost its focus. I noticed the end of my boarding pass peeking from the seat pocket and something moved me to stretch to it and pluck it out. Then I bent to the briefcase at my feet and I slipped the boarding pass in. My face grew tight from the angle forward and maybe that was my brain juicing up again because I grew suddenly conscious of this gesture. My habit as a flier was always to abandon my boarding pass in the seat pocket, but I was saving this one, I realized. Air France, JFK

to Charles De Gaulle. A. Dickerson. She flies to make love to
A. Bouchard for the first time. She flies to the rest of her life.
The boarding pass was a collectible. As was the moment of
touching Missy's head. The touch of her hand in return. My
phantom book-bid in East Hampton and dinner at Fellini's.
Lamplight in a Manhattan street and the brownstones in the
shadows. A Dalí Mary and child. Max's hands, and Fred's. My
nipples rising to Alain's touch. A terra-cotta lion. The sweet silence of my office stuffed with reference books. Molly leaping
into my arms and clinging. Maggie's conspiratorial wink. Two
hundred and sixty thousand dollars for a mediocre Renoir.
Mama setting her mouth hard at Daddy's painting, her eyes
filling with tears. The painting itself, however, was sold off
from the collection that is Amy Dickerson. Traded, actually,
for that moment with my sister.

And inside my briefcase, the boarding pass was pressed
against the folder that held my job offer, and the offer, as well,
of a piece of Alain's company. I'd still not signed, though it
occurred to me to do that now. I thought how I'd gain two things
at once, one inside the other, like buying a beautiful Victorian
fall-front desk only to find a hidden drawer within, holding an
extra treasure. Holding what? I burrowed into the pillow, closed
my eyes. A jewel, say. A desk and a jewel. My career and a piece
of this lovely man's career. Something like that. But this whole
metaphor was starting to cloy at me and I let it go. Though I
was still overheated, thinking, I'll sign it with him beside me. I
remembered his handwriting on the envelope he'd left on my
desk, the flexible fountain pen nib he'd used. I would use his

own vintage pen and I'd sign it on the bed while he lay naked beside me. For now, though, I simply wanted to sleep.

But I didn't.

My brain hummed on with the Rolls-Royce engines out on the wing and I thought about connoisseurs, those dear people who obsessed around in the center of my life. About how much they knew of the things they wanted. How much I ended up knowing in response to them. And how obsessed I myself was, as a result. Those engines out there in the dark, for example. I was sleepless and flying to my lover-to-be and what was most important was my momentum up here over the ocean, how I was being flung into my future. But instead, my—what?—this was an odd feeling now—my sense of engagement with the world, my confidence and my ease, my very sense of self—all these seemed somehow to reside in my knowing the names of these engines. The captain had mentioned their names, and I realized if I knew the type and the substance of their turbine blades, if I knew their horsepower and their thrust rating, I'd add all that to my experience of them at this moment and I'd be even more settled here and content and confident in the future. In short, I'd know them in the way of a connoisseur.

But I opened my eyes. The cabin was dim. Strangers were all around me, sleeping. I closed my eyes again. A chill came from the window. My mind would not hold still. I understood something of connoisseurs. I was one of them. Even just knowing the engines out there in the dark were made by Rolls-Royce, simply that, for all the self-assurance it gave me, it also held me

at a distance from them, kept me apart from what they were
most essentially giving me. The way I doted on the world—to
name it, find its value—I tried to put it off for a moment. So I
could sleep. Surely sleep was the opposite of naming and as-
sessing. It was a letting go. Drift. Somewhere else. The look in
Daddy's eye. The banging of the gavel to buy myself—just the
sound in that moment of self-possession—the popping of the
tent in the breeze. All the connoisseurs I knew lived at a distance. In some crucial way they lost touch with the very things
they loved, even as they knew more and more about them. These
were the thoughts humming behind my closed eyes. Somebody
said—a Frenchman, in fact, I think—that truly to see is to forget the name of the thing one sees. I wished now to forget.

Which is also to sleep.

But I did not sleep at all the night and morning I went to
Paris.

It was well past one in the afternoon when I finally emerged
from customs into the shoal of placards and hopeful faces
of the arrival hall at Charles De Gaulle. I was wheeling a
suitcase and a Rollaboard behind me and I was dazed, and then
I saw Alain, standing back from the crowd and solitary as a
monument, and I realized I'd never seen him any way but this,
in a perfectly tailored dark suit and white shirt and tie—this
one was a deep burgundy—and he saw me and smiled and his
hands opened at his sides and turned their palms to me. I understood this was the moment I was to run to him—I sensed his
gesture was asking for that—but I was tired and I was pulling

luggage, and I stopped. Alain picked up on it at once. Without turning to look, he raised one hand and made a gesture to someone behind him. Instantly a chauffeur appeared and cut a wide berth around Alain and came to me, murmuring a request in French to take my bags. I let them go to him, and Alain was still standing, smiling, and I was free to run.

I walked. Which was just fine. He took the last few steps toward me and I was in his arms. "I missed you very much," he said.

"Me too," I said and I lifted my face to him and he kissed me, but discreetly, on each cheek. I realized that in light of this simple bussing, even our embrace could be interpreted as platonic—we were not touching at the crotch, though I was limp enough in his arms that this was clearly his choice.

And he read my mind. He whispered, "Later, my darling, you will have my fullest feelings. I'm known in public."

"Of course," I said.

Then he took my arm at the elbow and he guided me outside and into a Mercedes stretch, guarded by a gendarme who tipped his hat first to me and then to Alain, and we were inside the darkened windows, and now we kissed, deep and long and, I'm afraid, for my part, tongue-tired. We ended the kiss and I tried to read his mind.

"I'm sorry," I said. "I'm very weary. I didn't sleep at all on the plane."

"Of course," he said, scooping me closer to him. I laid my head on his chest. "Rest now," he said. "I'll take you to the hotel and you should sleep until dinner tomorrow, yes?"

"Yes," I said.

I even slept, at last, curled against him. Then he was gently stroking me awake, touching my hair, my cheek, drawing his fingertip across my lips.

And so I found myself at the Ritz. The door clicked shut behind the bellman and I stood in the center of the floor of my room and my head began to buzz in recognition. Louis XVI all around. The furniture dazzled with marquetry and sinuous lines and cabriole legs and borders of laurel and acanthus leaves and lyres and swans, and there was a touch of the provinces, as well, a chair whose cabriole ended in a goat's foot, a commode of solid walnut. I was trying not to see all of this in my reflexive way, but it was difficult. Alain was thoughtful and generous and oh so apt in his choice of a place for me in Paris, but it was suddenly giving me a headache. So I stripped and slid into the bed and I was gone for a long while, rising finally to pee and it was dark and then I couldn't go back to sleep. It was past midnight, so I ate a room-service salad and some pâté and I stared at CNN for long while, trying to bore myself back to sleep, which finally happened somewhere along there in the early morning, and when I woke again, the telephone was ringing.

I reached to the phone and made a sleep-laden grunt and it was Alain's voice. "I woke you."

"Not quite yet," I said.

"Should I call back?"

"No. I'm coming around even as we speak."

"Are you naked, my darling?" he asked.

My mind was still a little slow and I thought about this for a moment and then my head rolled to the side to see. In my stretching to the phone I found my breasts were indeed naked and the rest was, no doubt, as well, and instinctively I pulled the sheet up to cover me. "I seem to be," I said.

"In two hours time I will come to you, and we have two options. You can remain naked and we'll order room service. Or I have reservations at a fine little Algerian restaurant."

"Which meal would that be?" I asked.

"Why, dinner of course. You've followed my suggestion— the best thing for a sleepless flight and jet lag, and months of too much hard work also, I suspect. It's five in the afternoon of the next day."

I made a whoa-there-cowboy face into the empty room. I'd been riding the range pretty hard in the past weeks—the past years, to tell the truth—but that seemed like a pathological lot of sleep. "I need to land on the planet before taking off again," I said. "Algerian first, naked later."

"Very well," he said, gently, but with a faint dip of disappointment in his voice. "Should I arrange another wake-up call?"

"No," I said. "I'm fine."

Which I wasn't, quite. I slept an hour and a quarter more and then had to race around to be ready for Alain, telling myself all the while that this awkward, displaced thing I was feeling was to be expected, considering. Mama and Missy and Daddy's stuff. An international flight and no sleep. Half a dozen time zones. A very strange few weeks. And imminent intimacy at last with Alain.

But the strangeness persisted. I was conscious of myself, throwing on a sweet little black shift with fringe at the bottom. It struck me that I never really thought about clothes. I dressed off-the-rack—mostly Armani and Prada—and my instincts were good but somewhat perfunctory. I probably should look at clothes the way I do all the other objects of the world. But I never have. Clothes turn into a kind of second skin. The clothes you wear have rarely had a life apart from you. What interests me is all the stuff we acquire that's been part of the lives of others before us. Stuff you've got to keep seeking out, even once you own it, you've got to go over to it and touch it or hold it or stare at it, stuff that doesn't just walk around with you, stuff you've got to find a place to keep and you have to walk away from it and then return to it. I'm interested in the choices we make about stuff like that. Auctionable stuff. Jackie Kennedy's pillbox hat, maybe. Marilyn Monroe's party dress. Ella Fitzgerald's shoe. That's clothing of interest to me, if it's your heart's desire to own it and you buy it to keep apart from you. But the stuff I put on my body—I don't know. I want to be pretty, of course. But dressed now with no conscious planning, I stood in the center of my room at the Ritz, and Alain was waiting downstairs, and I thought, I *am* pretty. Or not. Whichever, he wanted me and I wanted him. I looked at my hands. I would touch him and we would be naked, no clothes, no objects, either, but hands and legs and arms and tongues and a thing or two to fit together.

I shook my head to clear it.

After all the sleep I felt as muddled as I was on the plane. Had the uproar of these past weeks turned me slightly, permanently, mad?

Alain was waiting. Paris was waiting. I was waiting.

So I moved to the door, caught myself, and returned to my briefcase on a tulipwood marquetry table by the window. I took the agreements from the Groupe Bouchard S.A. packet, folded them neatly, and put them in my purse. I crossed the room again and went out and down the hall and down the elevator and along the Persian rug edged in imperial-purple and through the revolving door and into the vast brick expanse of the Place Vendôme with its great arc of hip-roofs and pilasters.

The Mercedes was there. The chauffeur was standing at the back and recognized me at once and opened the door. I moved forward, not knowing if Alain was inside or not until his hand appeared, white cuffed, but the rest of him made invisible by the shadows and my angle of approach. His hand floated there palm up, inviting me, as if only it had come to take me to dinner.

A nd so we kissed our way into the nineteenth arrondissement. Some trivial talk, as well, after kissing and before kissing—Cairo was hot and Houston was hot and his business went well and my auction went well and we missed each other and we both understood about the awkwardness of phones and so it was all right how few times we spoke by phone while we were apart—but mostly we kissed, and there were fleeting glimpses of Paris out the car window, but no flashes of recognition, mostly plane trees and horse chestnuts and building facades, clearly Paris, but far away and flitting past.

Then we sat, Alain and I, in a restaurant and we ate and drank, and this was very familiar suddenly, Alain and I across a table, speaking of food and wine, naming these things. The place was small and full of cigarette smoke that drifted to us and hung around the candle on our table and swarthy men slouched together at the small bar and Alain explained the cuisine, not Algerian in the strictest sense but *pied-noir,* from the French who'd been born in North Africa and grew up there and then were exiled, and their food was a mix of French and Arab and Spanish and Italian and Jewish. The waiter brought a brass mortar and pestle and set it in the center of the table—to collect the bones and the skin and the gristle of the meal, Alain said—and we drank pastis in tall glasses with ice and water and then we ate a platter of hor d'oeuvres—olives and carrots and fennel and chickpeas and artichokes in lemon juice and chilled sardines fried in garlic and pepper and cumin and cloves and paprika and vinegar. The sardines were called scabech. The whole platter was amuse-gueule—it means "make your face happy," Alain said. And if these pieds-noirs were cooked with more of an Italian touch or a Jewish touch, then the platter would also have *taiba,* chilled tuna with chilies and tomatoes, he said. But these pieds-noirs didn't.

"Is your face happy?" he asked me as the waiter whisked away the empty platter and I demurely slipped a sardine bone into the mortar.

"Yes," I said. The truth was, I felt oddly restless. I figured I'd made the wrong choice. Perhaps naked and room service would have been better. Though I wasn't quite sure why.

"Pied-noir. Do you know what that is?"

"No. Black feet?"

"Literally, yes. In the early nineteenth century, we took our North African colonies and our soldiers wore black boots.

The Arabs were all barefoot and these boots struck them as very strange when our soldiers marched in and they called out, 'Pieds-noirs!' So you see?"

"I do see."

"You understand the French language very well, yes?"

"Not so well, I think."

"I think you do, my darling," he said. "It is difficult for a Frenchman, you know, about his language. We are instructed in school very harshly. Like in many of my businesses, there is always intimidation. We are made to feel very stupid from a young age if we do not grasp the nuances of this very complex language. Your language is complex, as well, but you are very tolerant of the usage, I think. Your intellectuals even delight in taking up the language of the barefooted ones, so to speak."

"Isn't language mostly a matter of naming things?" I said. "We like names in English, the more the better."

"Perhaps," he said, and the waiter returned now with a bouillabaisse-couscous and lamb chops with poached eggs on top and lying on a bed of tomatoes and eggplant. "The name of this is chouchouka," Alain said, lifting a chop onto my plate.

I ate and Alain spoke of his language some more—the fear it strikes in the hearts even of Frenchmen. "I often disagreed with the man's politics," Alain said, "but I greatly admired François Mitterrand as a man, particularly as a man who was not afraid to use the imperfect subjunctive mood in public. Even, how you say, off the cuff. This takes courage, my darling."

He laughed softly at his own observation and offered his hand across the table. I took it. The lamb was very nice. The wine, too, though my mind had drifted when he'd told me what it was and I hadn't had the courage to ask again. It was red. I was growing sleepy once more.

"I remember his mistress and their daughter at his funeral," I said.

Alain nodded and let my hand go. "It was very passionate and dignified all at once," he said.

I suppose. Mitterrand felt like a collector to me, somehow.

"And he kept his cancer from the public all through his presidency," Alain said.

"Would it have taken more courage to speak of the cancer than in the imperfect subjunctive?" I said.

Alain laughed. "No. Less so. By far. He would have had our sympathy from the disease. To speak the language incorrectly, too many of us would have expected his knuckles to be rapped."

Alain leaned back in his chair and spread his hands, which spread his shoulders, which showed the fountain pen in his shirt pocket.

"May I see your pen?" I asked.

The non sequitur—and perhaps all the talk of language—made him mutter in French, a thing he'd rarely done with me. "Mais oui," he said and he plucked the pen from his pocket and handed it across the table.

I knew about fountain pens from an auction a couple of years ago. This was a large, handsome pen from 1930, a Waterman Patrician—arguably the finest Waterman marque. It was a color they'd called onyx, a dark cream with burgundy marbling and burgundy tips at either end, and there was a gold art deco band at the base of the cap—a multitude of tight little vertical cutouts with pin-dots at top and bottom. Alain's pen was in fine condition, though its cap was a few shades darker than the barrel, quite common for these pens.

"I write with the pens I collect," Alain said, as if completing the thought in my head. It was use that darkened the caps. He said, "I like to find excellent examples but I also rather like a trace of the dead man who valued the thing before me."

"Provenance," I said.

"Even not quite so worked out as that. I don't know who he was, the man who bought that pen seventy years ago, but I am content with the darkening of the pen from all the words he wrote."

Some tightness in me let go at this sentiment. I liked this in Alain.

I gently unscrewed the cap and the gold nib was enormous, flaring wide and then arrowing down to a fine point. I pressed the tip against my thumbnail and the nib flared, leaving a spot of burgundy ink.

"I love flexible nibs," he said.

I realized I was focusing intently on this object now and I felt calm at last—this was who I was after all—and I hoped the weirdness that had begun on the plane and had carried through the Ritz and this meal was at an end. I circled back to the thought of signing my papers beside him in the bed. This was the perfect object for the task. I angled the nib into the light. I knew the words I'd find engraved there—I'd sold a turquoise-and-gold Patrician pen and pencil set for three thousand dollars in the auction—and I saw the familiar "Patrician" etched into the gold, and "Waterman's Ideal."

I looked up at Alain. His eyes were on my hands, one of which held the cap of his pen, the other the barrel. After a moment he lifted his eyes to mine but I drew him back to my hands. I angled the cap slightly upward, showing the dark opening of it, and I worked the barrel forward between my fingers so that it seemed to emerge there from my hand, the lovely marbled barrel, and I drew it close to the cap and it went gently in. I turned it once, twice, a third time and it held tight.

I looked at Alain and he was fixed intently on the joined pen held at either end in my two hands. And he was wide-eyed. I felt like giggling. But I kept my face straight and I let go with the cap hand and with my fingertips at the very end of the barrel I let the pen turn upward, slowly, until it was upright before his face. This was Paris, after all, and so I softened my voice into an après-amour purr. "Nice pen," I said.

It was dark. It was past ten. We stepped out of the restaurant and immediately into the limousine. We slid away and this was starting to feel very familiar, too, making out with Alain in a car behind black-tinted windows. Only now, the distant scroll of lights and shadows was Paris.

The making out was nice, though. I thought of Alain's fountain pen—that is, how he liked the signs of some unknown, long-dead man writing with it—a businessman, likely, for the Patrician had been an expensive pen—and as I touched Alain's tongue with mine, his lips with mine, this was the focus of my ardor, his regard for the faintest traces of a past human life found on a beautiful object.

His hand went eventually to my breast and we kissed some more as he stroked me into life there, and with the hand he also posed a question that finally we paused for him to ask. He did it indirectly. "Are you interested in a bistro or such tonight?" It was clear from his voice that he wasn't.

As for me, I was still weary. And I was, frankly, wet. I was ready to make love at last to Alain Bouchard. "Not tonight," I said.

"Good," he said, and his strong left arm drew me tightly to him as he pushed the intercom button and said to the chauffeur, "The Ritz."

This surprised me a little, the assumption that we'd do this at my hotel. I pulled away slightly from his embrace to explore this. "The hotel?" I said.

"Yes? Isn't it good, the room?"

"Of course. But it's so neutral."

"It's the *Ritz,* n'est-ce pas?"

"I'd love to go where you live," I said.

"It's not so nice as the Ritz."

"But it's *you.*"

He thought this over for a moment, looking at me carefully. We were passing through residential streets and the spill of light into the car was meager. I could not see his face to read it. Then he said, "Of course. I must become accustomed to this. You know exactly the right thing to do."

Which was more or less the right thing to say. He touched the intercom button and he spoke low and quickly to the chauffeur, but I heard a quai address, and then I returned to my place in the crook of his arm. We rode in silence. There'd been no sarcasm in his voice—none that I could detect—when he'd complimented my sense of the right thing, but I was vaguely troubled by having to persuade him to take me to the place where he lived in Paris.

"Are you sure this is all right?" I said.

He drew me closer. "Of course. I'm sorry I didn't think to invite you at first. I'm not so very much at home there anymore. It has certain associations. Do you understand?"

I suddenly did. Past lives. He preferred his fountain pen's long-dead anonymous businessman to the wife—or wives— who'd shared the apartment. "Listen . . ." I began.

He cut me off. "No. You're right. You will make my own apartment new for me."

"Are you sure?"

"I'm sure."

I burrowed in and the silence now was a sweet silence, a placid waiting for the time and the place of our first deep intimacy.

And drifting by through these blackened windows were lamplight and tree shadow and a dark sense of an unbroken four-story run of facades. I reminded myself this was Paris. Perhaps I *didn't* know exactly the right thing to do. Perhaps we needed Paris first, Alain and I. But I'd heard the preference in his voice, driven by his desire for me. It was my preference too.

I turned my eyes from the window. I touched his hand.

Paris could wait.

He palmed my elbow and we were across the pavement and I glanced over my shoulder at the hunkered back end of Notre Dame, lit bright down the Seine, and we crossed Alain's lobby and entered an ironwork elevator. The door clanked shut and we began to creak upward. Abruptly his hands were on my shoulders and he turned me around to face him and he pressed me close and kissed me and I had my own associations, I realized—in this case, with elevators—and it soured the moment for me. But he expected no more from me for now; we simply pressed and kissed until the car heaved to a halt. He let go and drew the iron door back and then we were at his apartment door with a scrolled brass knob in the center.

I went in before him.

As who, exactly?

I stopped in his foyer. All about me were objects of rarity and provenance, and of course the usual me was ready to read them. But I held back from that.

There was the me of my body, of my sexuality—I found I was holding her back, too, in spite of the after-touch tremolo on my lips, my tongue, my throat, my eyelids. She was here to determine a value as well, for herself and for this man. But not yet. Not quite yet.

And there was the me I'd bid up and won that afternoon in East Hampton. Her intent in this place was less clear, though I sensed that she was the one who'd actually brought us here. I would let her lead us forward now, but she did not know what step to take.

The touch of Alain's hand was on the small of my back. And the gentlest pressure to go ahead.

I did.

I emerged into a wide living room. Before me was a wall of windows open to the night. I saw only a scattering of light in distant treetops and on dark angled roofs, but I knew there was some big thing just out of sight in between, and if I'd only take a step and another and more and cross this room, I could see it.

But then it was Amy Dickerson in the window. A chandelier had flared and the room blazed around me and I could see her, caught in the plane of glass, distant, startled, standing alone in my black dress, my hair gilded with the light and falling about my face. And then there was movement near me in that distant image. A body crossing. I stiffened and gasped as if I were watching a horror movie and this Amy Dickerson on the screen was preoccupied and disoriented and unaware of the creature rushing at her. Alain. I made myself recognize him and he drew near and he was behind me, though I knew this only from the image before me. He put a hand on my shoulder, my right shoulder, and I started. It was the opposite shoulder from the one I'd expected from the image. I turned my face to him sharply.

"I'm sorry," he said. "I didn't mean to startle you."

"No," I said. "It's nothing."

"I gave us light."

And I looked away from him and I was abruptly aware of the room. It was the Ritz again. Louis XVI. Only more of it. Perhaps he'd assumed we'd make love at the hotel because he himself would have felt at home there. My eye went to a chair near to me, early Louis XVI, still not comfortable with what it was becoming. The chair had Louis XVI legs—straight-edged, fluted, tapering to a scroll foot—but its curved, heart-shaped back was strictly Rococo. I wrenched my mind away from the chair. I was uncomfortable, too, moving from lover to appraiser—or perhaps appraiser to lover—and I turned my face to the inner wall, to the marble fireplace, and there was Venus.

She was as Alain had described her. She sat holding her lute beneath her naked breasts and her face was lifted and Cupid was leaning on her thigh. But there was more. She was a slightly fleshy, blandly pretty sixteenth-century girl—a real-seeming girl, a girl I felt I knew at once—and her face was raised—in song, as Alain had said? Perhaps. But I wasn't seeing her that way. It wasn't just her face that was lifted, so were her eyes, and her eyes had a sparkle in them as they yearned upward, and her lips were parted only slightly, not nearly enough for singing but just right for the feeling that was clearly present in her eyes—something like awe, like rapture. And Cupid was leaning against her but he was staring at the rose in the lute's center. He stared quite lovingly at it and with a sense of naughty secretiveness, as if he were gazing upon his goddess's luit, her very pussy.

I moved toward her and angled my head slightly, just as hers was. Her hands were curved delicately, one around the neck of the instrument, the other—thumb and forefinger parted, about to pluck—just beneath the rose.

Alain had followed me to her, for his hands were suddenly on my shoulders. "Come," he said.

He turned me with his hands, gently moved me forward to the corridor that began to the right of the fireplace. I let him direct me and my eyes came down from Venus and I stopped, resisted the press of him for a moment as my eyes fell on a lute.

It was leaning against the fireplace jamb. It was the lute in the painting above. It was the lute leaning in almost exactly the same place in my own apartment.

"You have a lute," I said.

"Perhaps one day we will play a duet," he said.

"Do you play?"

"No," he said, pressing me forward again.

I yielded and we went into the dim plushness of the corridor and I heard a click behind me and the corridor abruptly darkened with the extinguishing of the living room lights. We passed an open door and I glanced into his office: a massive desk in shadow, a yellow puddle at its corner from a green-shaded library lamp.

His hands felt heavy on me. The lute was propped up inside my head and I couldn't put it aside. And Venus was in there, too, her mouth parted slightly as if she wanted to speak. Other doors passed. They were closed. There was a scrabbly thing going on somewhere in my chest. Too high up to be sexual. Unease, it was. I didn't know why. But the dark heaviness of his office lingered in me. And it threw my mind back to the living room and its elaborate eighteenth-century dazzle. He'd been wrong, of course, when he'd said his place was not so nice as the Ritz. And he knew it. The fact was, he hadn't wanted me here. Even now. He wanted to fuck me in my hotel room.

We approached the bedroom door. There was a small, piss-yellow lamp going in there, as well. I could see the floral garlands of a footboard. Louis XVI again.

I needed time to think.

We were in the bedroom. It smelled the faintly mildewy

smell of old wood. We were surrounded by furniture and I did not look at it. The headboard of the bed was massive, walnut and cane, edged in carved acanthus leaves and pinecones.

Alain turned me at the foot of the bed and he embraced me, hard, and pressed his mouth onto mine. I kissed him and he did the hard and then soft and then hard again rhythm thing he seemed to like, and when he finally let our lips part, I drew back a little before he could leap in again.

"Darling," I said. He'd called me darling plenty already and I wanted his full and sympathetic attention. "Can we make love at first light? I'm very tired and we've waited this long and we've both wanted it to be perfect, haven't we?"

He hesitated for a moment, his brow furrowing faintly.

"What's the opposite of an aubade?" I said.

He smiled.

"Two lovers coming together for the first time at daybreak," I said.

"We will have to invent the word for ourselves," he said.

"Dawnfuck," I said. "For violin and saxophone."

He laughed.

"I'm very tired myself, my darling," he said. "Let's sleep beside each other first. Yes." He let go of me and drew back a few steps.

"Yes."

"But can we at least be naked?" he said.

I hesitated, but he didn't notice. Instantly his coat was off and his tie and his hands were working their way down the buttons on his shirt. He was facing me still, having only taken those two or three steps back and not turned away. I was struggling a little with a weird and uncharacteristic attack of shyness before a man I was determined to sleep with. I kicked off my shoes. That was a safe beginning. Alain's shirt was off and then his sleeveless undershirt—odd, it struck me, for him to be wearing an undershirt in the heat—and his chest was bare and aswirl with dark hair. He was wrenching at his belt and still not turning and I figured he must have a big penis, since he was so anxious to be full-frontal naked for me.

"You're waiting," he said. "Good."

I *was* waiting, as a matter of fact. But as hazy as its motive was for me, I didn't think my hesitation was a good thing. Nor was it a good thing that he thought it was a good thing. I was expected to perform for him after *he* was naked.

His pants were down but they were suddenly stuck. He'd forgotten his shoes and he toed them off and his pants were free and he kicked them aside and he hopped on one foot and then the other, rolling off his black dress socks, and without a pause he grabbed his boxer shorts at the waist and stripped them down.

What is it in a collector that the passion focuses on one thing and not another? Silver teapots but not water pitchers. Pocket watches but not wristwatches. Tiffany lamps but not Handel. Or the other way around. I myself have always focused on the hands of the men I've been with. Penises are distinctive, certainly, and I daresay there's many a woman who, in those special times of a collector's reflection, sits in tranquility and examines the images in her head of her past lovers' penises, the special wrinklings and bends and textures of them. I prefer hands.

But when Alain tossed his underpants aside and struck a naked my-chest's-a-barrel-my-arms-are-thick-my-pot-is-minimal pose before me, and given my earlier suspicion based on the alacrity of his disrobing, I was surprised at how ordinary his penis was. Not rare. Not of an ideal size, though neither was he in full readiness and I suppose there was some wiggle room here in my estimation of him. Not that it mattered to me, of course. And he did have extraordinary hands. But what *was* his rush, then, to be naked? Did he *think* what he was showing me was not ordinary? And how was it that I came to be in this frame of mind? Was I pondering making a bid on his intimacy? Perhaps.

He was waiting.

I felt a fluttering going on—again unpleasantly higher in my body than it was supposed to be—this one all the way up into my throat like incipient nausea. I was tired, I told myself. I'd eaten Algerian things. It wasn't Alain causing my weirdness. I pressed on. I crossed my arms in front of me and grabbed my dress just below the waist and stripped it up and off, quickly—*whatever* it was causing this ickiness, I wanted to be done with this moment and then try to make it up to Alain at dawn. I was struck by how nearly naked I'd been to start with. Already there were only my panties left and Alain was breathless and gaping before me, his eyes riveted on my breasts, taking me in, and for all this ardor about my body, he'd been patient, certainly, for this moment over the past weeks, and I liked him for that and I liked him for the ardor, too, though this was more a thought than a feeling. I was still uneasy. And I understood his rush now. It wasn't about me seeing his body. It was about *him* watching *me.* Great. That should make me feel sexy and appreciated, but all I was prompted to do was try to keep my panties on. I turned toward the bed. But Alain stopped me with a word.

"Please," he said. I faced him again. "Please," he said with great tenderness and desire and he nodded at my panties.

Okay, I said to myself, making my voice sound in my head. Okay, do this thing. It wasn't so long ago he was making you wet down there and he was making you think about the rest of your life being ahead of you and he was convincing you quite easily that he was an exceptional man. You're horny and you're discriminating, okay, but this is going way too fucking far.

So I thumbed my panties down and the sudden sense of open air on my luit made me thrum a little and Alain was riveted on that part of me, like Cupid in the other room, though there was no sense of secretiveness or innocent naughtiness about it, this was an outright gobbly stare as I stepped out of the panties and dropped them beside me and faced him. I didn't like his expression at the moment and I glanced at him in the same place on his body and he was fully engaged now and still his penis was ordinary. On the low end of ordinary, actually, and I looked at his hands and they were clenched at his sides.

"To sleep, perchance to dream," I said and I turned abruptly away and darted to the bed and I stripped the covers down and slipped in. I lay on my side away from him, hoping not to offend him with the gesture. I wanted him. I'd wanted him for weeks. He'd said nothing, done nothing, to change that, surely. I couldn't think of a thing. But I put my back to him now and the mattress sagged with his entry and his warmth was nearby and I turned around to him. He was propped up on one arm, facing me, and he was massive, really, in this bed, this close, and he was ready to do this now, I knew, but I kissed him lightly on the lips and said, "Thank you."

He nodded and I lay down on my back and he settled in on his back, as well. I'd meant my thanks. I was grateful to him—I *liked* him—for his not pushing this right now, in spite of his erection. So what the hell was going on? Jet lag was going on. Exhaustion was going on. Only that, I thought, and one breath later I was asleep.

I sat up abruptly, the covers falling away from my naked breasts. It wasn't dawn, I knew, but for a moment I didn't know why that was significant. There was a phlegmy grinding in the room. A man's snore. I shook my head sharply back and forth and understood I was in Paris, in Alain's bed, and he was sleeping noisily beside me, preparing for the promise of first light. Across the room, on some piece of antique something-or-other, indistinguishable in the dark, the time crouched in red numerals. 12:11. I'd slept for only about an hour. I felt as queasy and displaced as ever. But I was wide awake.

I drew back the covers, very gently, and I rose from the bed without altering Alain's snore by so much as a single snaggle. I could see general shapes around me and I moved beyond the foot of the bed and I paused. My dress was somewhere on the floor, but the air felt nice on my body and I slipped out of the room and into the corridor still naked.

The silk nap of the runner chilled the soles of my feet and I went softly along without a purpose except to move the air against my body and to put a little distance between me and Alain and perhaps to sit and think things through for a time.

But I reached his office—the door still open, the lamp on the desk still on—and I stopped. I felt as if he were inside. The true Alain, apart from the limos and the restaurants and the bed down the hall. He'd *left* the door open and the light on. I realized he'd not expected to come back here with me tonight, but he still could have risen and closed this all off before he went to sleep, or even as we passed by the first time, just as he'd turned off the lights in the living room. He'd left the door open and the light on and I felt a little itchy again to touch him.

I wasn't being thick-headed about this. Alain was a sexually-active-teenager's-worth older than me. His temples were gray. So I was a sucker for the open invitation to enter his den.

Duh.

And maybe the confusion of all that, coming here more or less straight from Houston, was what was going on inside me. But that seemed way too simple.

I stepped into his study and now my nakedness was acute and I felt a little trembling in me, closer to the place it should be. Closer, but no cigar. I was jumpy, too. I didn't know how to approach this room. There were things around, nice things, furniture things. That's as far as I wanted to go. I wasn't going to appraise in the nude. But they were *his* things. He was a collector. If I wanted, in fact, to know this man better—know him as a man unlike any other—before letting him enter my body, then this was the place to examine.

I looked around. The desk was massive and functional, though inflected with Deco, and the bookshelves were built-in. But the rest still spoke of collecting—an Empire bureau plat, a tapestry fauteuil—and then my eyes fell on an odd piece, a large walnut linen press opposite the desk. It was probably early eighteenth century, but it had no drawers, only two double-paneled doors and a low, paneled base. It was most likely American and its lines were so simple and its personality so unassuming that I knew it had a special purpose in this room.

I crossed to it. A small brass key sat in its keyhole and my hand instinctively went to it and touched it, and I paused. This was wrong, of course, to snoop around in his furniture. But he wanted to snoop around inside my *body,* after all. I could still retreat if things seemed private in here.

I turned the key and pulled the door and it creaked sharply and I jumped back and I jerked my head to the office door and listened. There was nothing. I even thought I could faintly hear his snoring down the hall. I looked back to the linen press. There were boxes and books in the shadows. I grasped both doors, determined to get this over with. I opened them briskly and the creaking was quieter and they were wide open, and before I looked inside, I turned away and waited, listening to the rest of the apartment. Nothing.

I stepped forward.

There were three wide shelves and on the highest was a long row of stamp albums and on the second shelf was a stacking of fancy old tin boxes—chocolate and tobacco and biscuits—and on the bottom shelf were two wide, multidrawered fountain pen cases. These were his collections. His private collections, his intimate collections. I reached out to one of the tins—for Snake Charmer Cigarettes—and took it up and it was

heavy. I lifted the lid and turned to the light on the desk and
the tin was filled with ancient Roman coins in plastic holders.

I smiled. Collections within collections. He had the heart
of a little boy, squirreling away whatever struck his fancy. I
closed the lid. A wide-hipped Victorian beauty in a long dress
held a snake up to her face and one was wrapped around her
neck and another coiled at her feet. I put the box back and went
down the row a ways and picked up a Muratti "Young Ladies"
Cigarettes tin and a woman in a boater was enjoying a smoke on
the lid and I opened her up and inside were Potin Chocolate cards,
small turn-of-the-twentieth-century photo inserts of French au-
thors—George Sand, Jules Renard, Victor Hugo, Verlaine—and
I nearly laughed out loud. I realized that a moment ago, when
I saw him as a boy, I'd half expected to find baseball cards in
one of these tins. And this was close enough.

I closed the tin and put it back and now I felt ready to slip
down the hall and into his bed and prepare for the dawn. But I
thought of his pens and I crouched and reached to the bottom
shelf and pulled open a shallow drawer in one of the cases. It
was in my shadow and so I closed the drawer and drew the whole
case out. It was heavy, but manageable, and I placed it on the
floor beneath the spill of light. I opened the top drawer again.

His pens were beautiful. There were eight little velvet-
padded troughs in the drawer and each had a Parker eyedrop-
per pen—pens of gold and abalone and mother-of-pearl—I still
held my appraiser's instinct in check and I closed the drawer. I
opened another and it was full of continental safety pens—
Watermans mostly, worked over in Italy and Spain, covered
with intricately filigreed rolled gold and Toledo-work—and the

next drawer was full of Conklin crescent-filler pens—and the
next, Parker Duofolds—and I stopped. I closed the Duofold
drawer and didn't open another. I'd seen enough. And I thought
of his sweet attachment to his Waterman onyx Patrician. I wanted
to touch him again. I'd go back to bed.

But as I shifted around to get a grip on the pen case, just
enough light fell at just the right spot at just the right moment
for my glance to pick up an odd thing. On the inner wall of the
linen press, down by the bottom shelf, was an arcing scrape.

Okay. Not so odd. Now I understood the out-of-place piece
of American furniture. It had a hidden compartment beneath
the bottom shelf. I thumped back onto the floor to think. The
weave of the Aubusson rug was scratchy as hell on my bare butt.
That was okay. It was like a hair shirt. I needed to do a little
penance—of a preemptive sort—for what I was afraid I was
about to do.

Okay. He had a collection of something or other in there.
I should put the pens away and walk out of here.

But I believed—and he openly professed to believe—that
we are what we collect. So either I was going to be just fine with
whatever was in there and there was no harm done in snoop-
ing, or I was not going to be fine with it and I'd gladly live with
the guilt so that I didn't have to find out something nasty about
him the hard way, after I'd given him my body and—yes, it was
leading to that—my heart.

My butt had been uncomfortable enough for long enough.
I rose up into a crouch and drew out the other fountain pen
case and set it aside. Then I knelt before the linen press and
slipped my fingertips under the tiny lip of the shelf and I lifted.

The shelf went up easily, soundlessly, and there was darkness before me and I thought to turn on other lights in this room, but I was afraid of being found out, especially now. I twisted aside to let the light from the desk spill in, and I peered hard at the darkness, waiting for shapes to emerge.

There was only empty space, to my eye. I was ready to close the lid and get the hell back to bed, but then I saw something. Barely. It was lying low and flat in the dark. My hands trembled as I reached in. It was a long, wide book. Bound in leather. Okay. Not so bad. Surely there wasn't a book that could end this thing.

I didn't look at it at once. I rose and circled the desk with it in my arms and it was heavy and it was thick and I sat down in Alain's chair and laid the book before me on the desktop. There was soft leather now, soft as kid gloves, on my butt.

I looked at the book, and it wasn't a book at all. It was an album, with heavy black photo pages.

I made a quick sucking noise and held my breath. Reflex. My hands were on the desktop, palms down, and I pressed hard there, did not want to raise them. But I'd gone far in the past few weeks and I'd come back around to this, and now I willed myself to breathe, to draw the chair closer to the desk, to lift my hands and move them to the album, and I opened the cover.

The first page had four tipped-in photos. Suddenly a knot unraveled in my chest. Everything was fine. This was a family album. These were his sisters, perhaps. Cousins. Here were four young women, teenagers. Top left was a faintly blurry black-and-white, a lanky girl in a one-piece bathing suit with fluting at the bodice and she had a rope of braided hair hanging over one shoulder. She was standing at the wooded edge of a grassy slope that rolled down to a lake. Lettered neatly in white ink below: *Claire Reynard. 23 Juillet 1960.* And in French, the words *first time beneath this tree.* I didn't get it yet. But I looked at the next picture, a head-and-shoulder candid shot of a freckle-faced girl with a Santa Claus hat. *Marcelle ?? vers la fin de Décembre 1960.* And below her was a photo of a girl shot from above in fading color and she was sitting in front of a mirror in a bistro and she had a lovely, wide, toothy smile. *Solange Lamy 8 mois, 1961.*

And the thing I hadn't quite let sink in finally did. These were the girls he'd fucked. I opened a batch of pages, about a third of the way in, and a model lounged on the fender of a Citroen DS and she was Yvonne who Alain fucked for about a year from the summer of 1967 to the summer of 1968, and on the next page was a grouping of three Polaroids of three different women and their dates all overlapped with each other and with Yvonne's, and they were all variously naked—one with her blouse open, lifting her puffy nipples to the camera in what looked like the Tuileries; one naked in side-view with tight, small breasts, bending into a refrigerator and glancing at the camera with a faint look of surprise; another with long, wild hair lying back on a couch with one leg hooked up over the back and she was blowing a kiss to Alain behind the Polaroid. She was aware, it seemed, that he was in the process of remembering her heavily befurred pussy forever.

I sat back in the chair.

I didn't know what I was feeling about all this.

Jealous? Not exactly. Would Alain have reason to be jealous of the memories I have of my lovers' hands? He might, of

course. Men like to wipe away the past. But not Alain. He preserved the past. Here he was, collecting images of all the women
he'd fucked—no, to keep thinking of it as *fucking,* I was still struggling with something that had to do with *me*—*to fuck* is to take
the intimacy lightly and throw it off and not give it a place inside
you. He obviously was doing much more than that. He was not
just collecting images of these women here, he was collecting *them.*

Which somehow didn't make me feel any better.

I leaned forward and opened the book another batch of
pages and another. He was into preserving pussies for quite a
few years. And there were some portraits, too, clothed shots—
I presumed these were women who'd said no to the pussy-shots.
And then I jerked forward. I'd skipped ahead to a page near
the end and I was looking at a woman with her blond hair tied
up behind her and her breasts naked and her face lifted and
the lute in her lap. *Sybil Harlowe. 1995.* And I turned another
few pages at once and now there was a redhead, as wide-hipped
and well-fed as Venus herself, and she was Colleen and she was
the month of May in 1997 and her left hand was curved delicately around the neck of the lute and her right hand was about
to pluck a string near the rose, and I closed the album.

I suppose it's inevitable that an auctioneer comes to di-
vide the world into collectors and noncollectors. But it is a true
principle of my trade, as well, I think—especially in Paris, whose
cafes gave succor to the notion that we create ourselves in our
choices, our actions—it is true of an auctioneer in Paris to think
that we all either collect or we are collected. Alain would ask
me, one day, to pose for a special remembrance—something
to carry off to Cairo with him, he'd say, to meditate on through

the long nights at the Semiramis Inter-Continental. Please, he'd say, shrug off your clothes and take up the lute and lift your eyes to heaven. Let me take your picture. And if I'd given my body and my heart I could only say yes. And that's who Amy Dickerson would be.

So I rose now and I took up the album and I went to the linen press and I laid the book in the shadows. I closed the hidden compartment and placed the pen cases back on the shelf and I closed the doors and turned the key.

Then I slipped quietly, calmly, down the hall and found my panties and my dress and my shoes and my purse in the dark, even as Alain slept on, dreaming, perhaps, of all his women, and I covered my body and I went down the corridor and into his office one last time.

I sat at his desk and took out the Nichols and Gray agreements and I dug into my purse and I found a Bic Clic Stic made of smooth-molded plastic and containing 1.2 miles of ink, estimated value eighty-nine cents. And I clicked my Bic and signed the contracts and I took a piece of memo paper from a container on the desk and I wrote: *Alain, I will be much more valuable to you if I strictly remain the star of one of your properties.* I hesitated at "star," but in my world, that is, in fact, what I am, and I left it. I wrote, *I will enjoy owning a piece of you.* And I signed *Amy Dickerson* and squared up the contracts and the memo in the center of the desk, and I rose and I stepped out into the corridor. Down the way Alain was snoring on, and I turned and moved to the living room.

And I was struck motionless: the place was bright with the luminosity of Paris. I crossed the room, heading for the light and for what I'd sensed, but not seen, when I first came in. I slowed and stopped, and the tops of the plane trees were before me and below were the Haussmann streetlamps and the wall of the quai. And beyond was the thing I'd somehow missed for the thirty-some-odd hours I'd been in this city: the river. She was the wet, strong, independent center of Paris, and there was silence in my head at last and a sudden, quirky sense of purpose.

I stripped off my dress and I stripped off my panties and I laid my palms and my nipples and my forehead on the cool glass and I stared at the river as she took in the light from Paris and broke it up and put it back together and made it her own. I watched her and I watched her and we were alone together here, she and I.

And then a great white searchlight raced along the quai and up into my eyes, flaring silently on me, and I let go of the window with nipples and hands and face and the light was bright on my body and I heard the distant growl of a motor. Moving through the river, opening the long luit of water like a lover, was a bateau-mouche, its tourists making a late-night collection of the sights of Paris—the Grand Palais and the Place de la Concorde and the Tuileries and the Louvre and the Île St-Louis and Notre Dame and the facades of these apartment houses and this naked woman.

I pressed against the window again. I had not seen Paris yet this time round. I'd been caught in an old and wearying track so far, but now suddenly I *was* Paris. I waved. The bateau honked.

I stayed pressed there until the boat was gone and its wake had subsided and the river was self-possessed again, unchanged.

I felt a tender thing now for the Seine, for the trees and the lamps and the quai and the zinc roofs across the river and the cathedral burning down the way and the lights beyond. They were waiting for me. I'd walk alone through a Paris night to the Ritz and I'd collect myself along the way. I slipped my clothes back on and I took my first step, and as I did, I glanced toward Venus.

I understood now the look in her upturned face. She was alone in the world, but she was still rapturous with love. Even in the dim light I could see the twinkle in her eyes.